SHAKESPEARE

A MIDSUMMER NIGHT'S DREAM

RETOLD BY
NEL YOMTOV

ILLUSTRATED BY
BERENICE MUNIZ

COLORED BY
FARES MAESE

STONE ARCH BOOKS
a capstone imprint

Retold by Nel Yomtov
Illustrated by Berenice Muniz
Colored by Fares Maese

Series Editor: Sean Tulien
Editorial Director: Michael Dahl
Series Designer: Brann Garvey
Art Director: Bob Lentz
Creative Director: Heather Kindseth

Shakespeare Graphics is published by
Stone Arch Books, 151 Good Counsel Drive,
P.O. Box 669, Mankato, Minnesota 56002

WWW.CAPSTONEPUB.COM

Cataloging-in-Publication Data is available
at the Library of Congress website.

ISBN: 978-1-4342-2605-1 (library binding)
ISBN: 978-1-4342-3449-0 (paperback)

PRINTED IN THE UNITED STATES OF AMERICA IN
STEVENS POINT, WISCONSIN.
032011
006111WZF11

TABLE of CONTENTS

CAST OF CHARACTERS: .... PAGE 08

ACT 1: .... PAGE 10

ACT 2: .... PAGE 20

ACT 3: .... PAGE 34

ACT 4: .... PAGE 54

ACT 5: .... PAGE 62

SHAKESPEARE

WILLIAM SHAKESPEARE WAS ONE OF
THE GREATEST WRITERS THE WORLD
HAS EVER KNOWN.

HE WROTE COMEDIES, TRAGEDIES,
HISTORIES, AND ROMANCES ABOUT
ANCIENT HEROES, BLOODY WARS,
AND MAGICAL CREATURES.

THIS IS ONE OF THOSE STORIES . . .

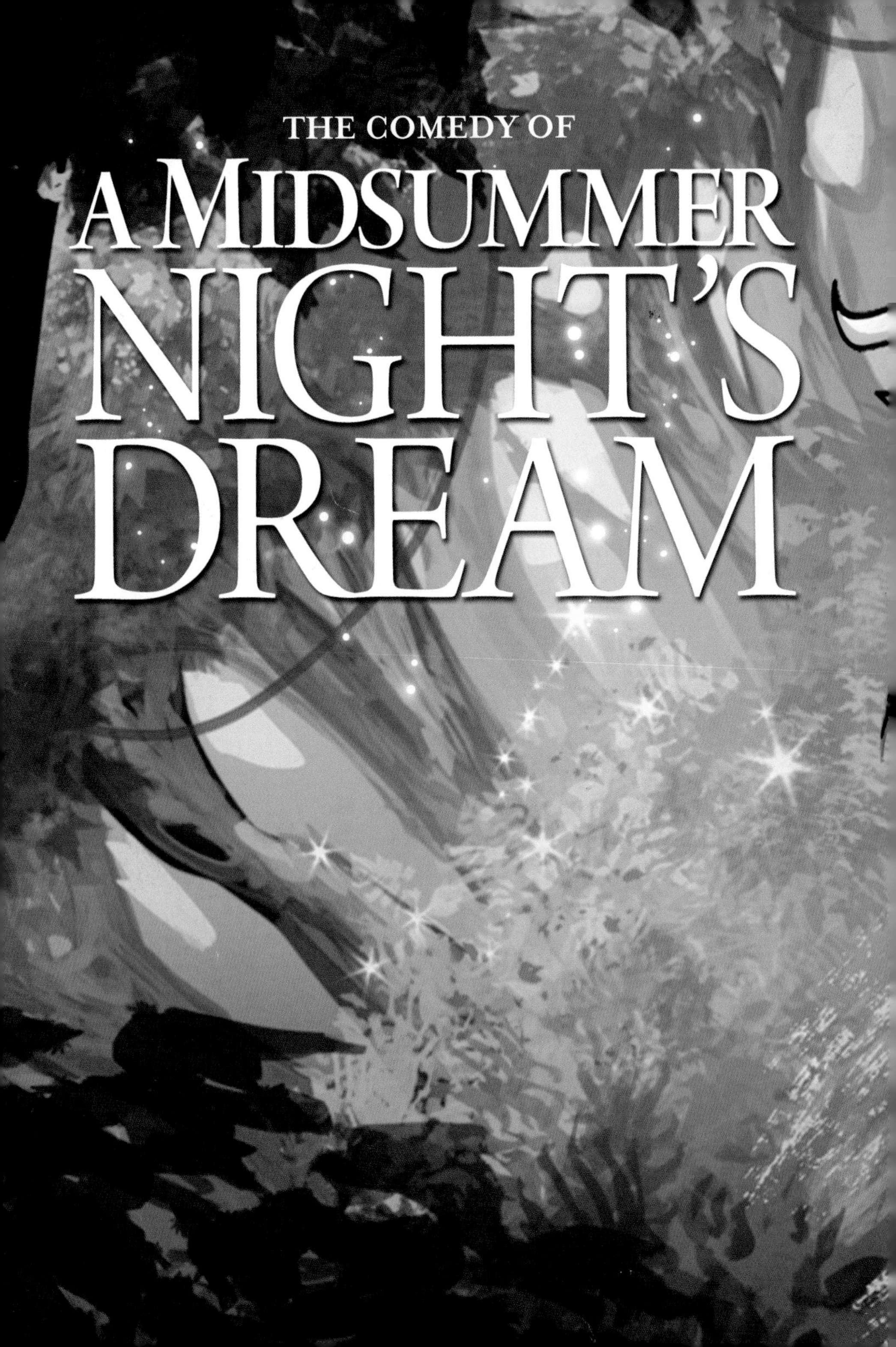
THE COMEDY OF
A MIDSUMMER
NIGHT'S
DREAM

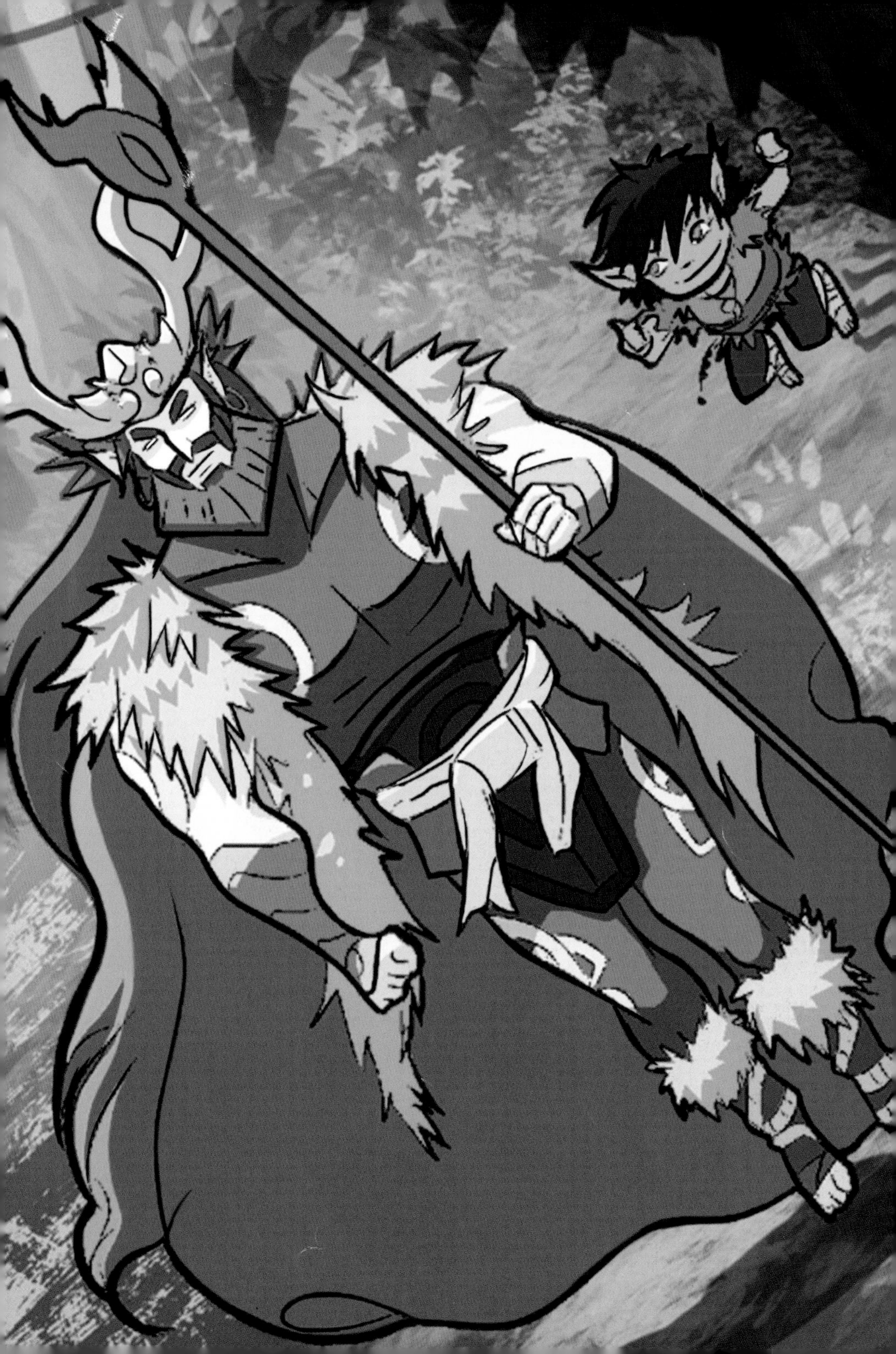

THE CAST

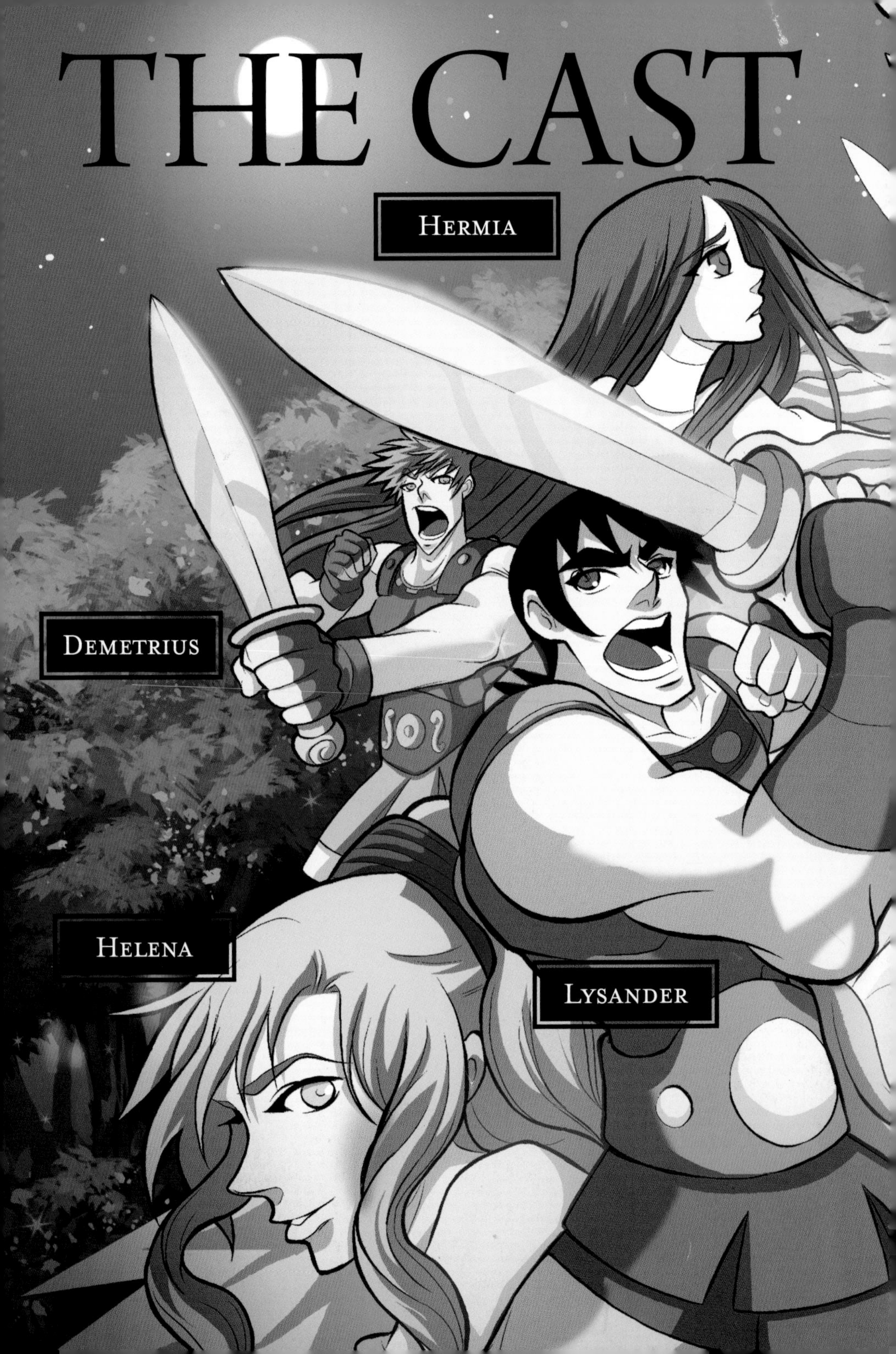
HERMIA
DEMETRIUS
HELENA
LYSANDER

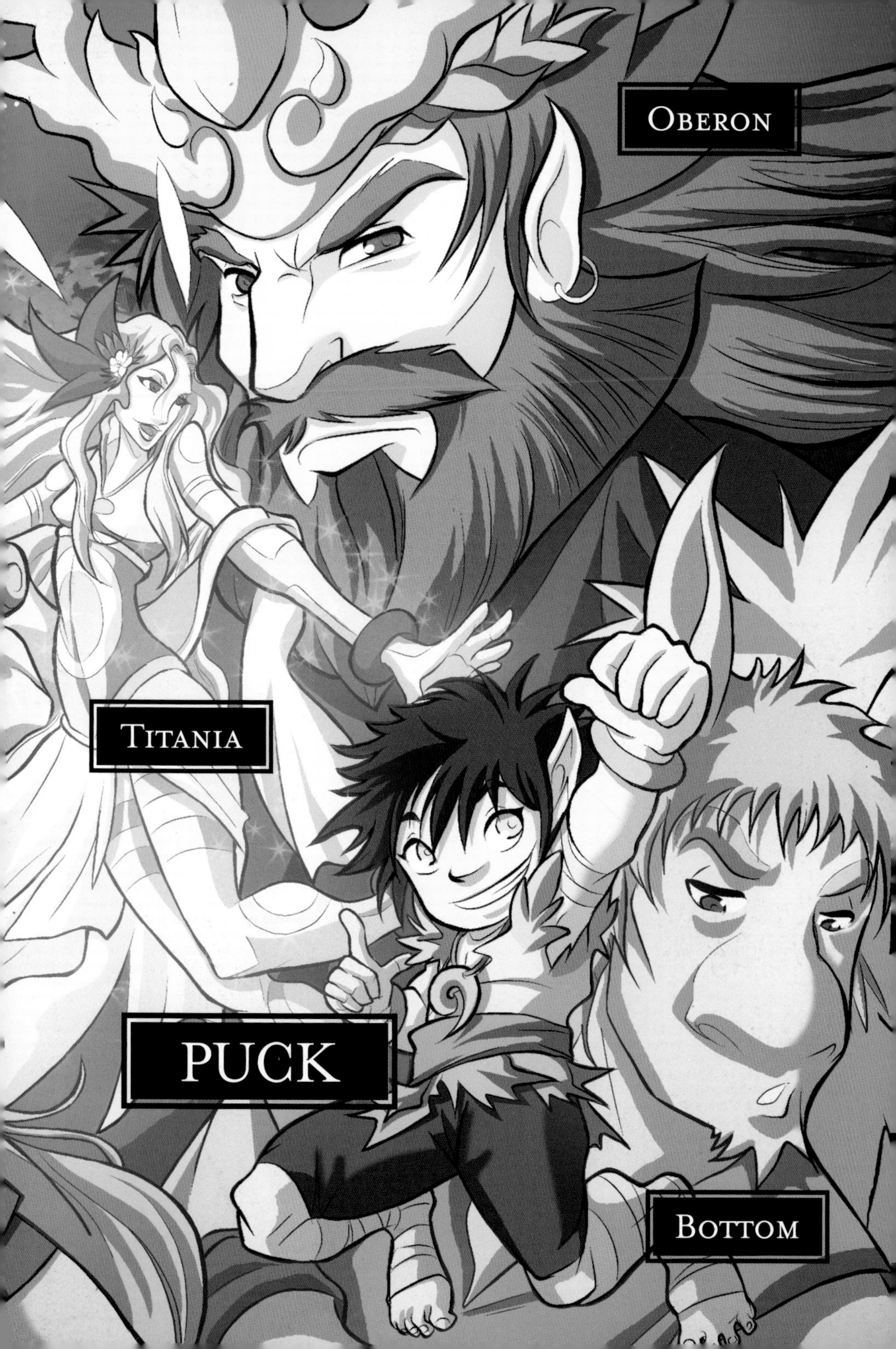
OBERON
TITANIA
PUCK
BOTTOM

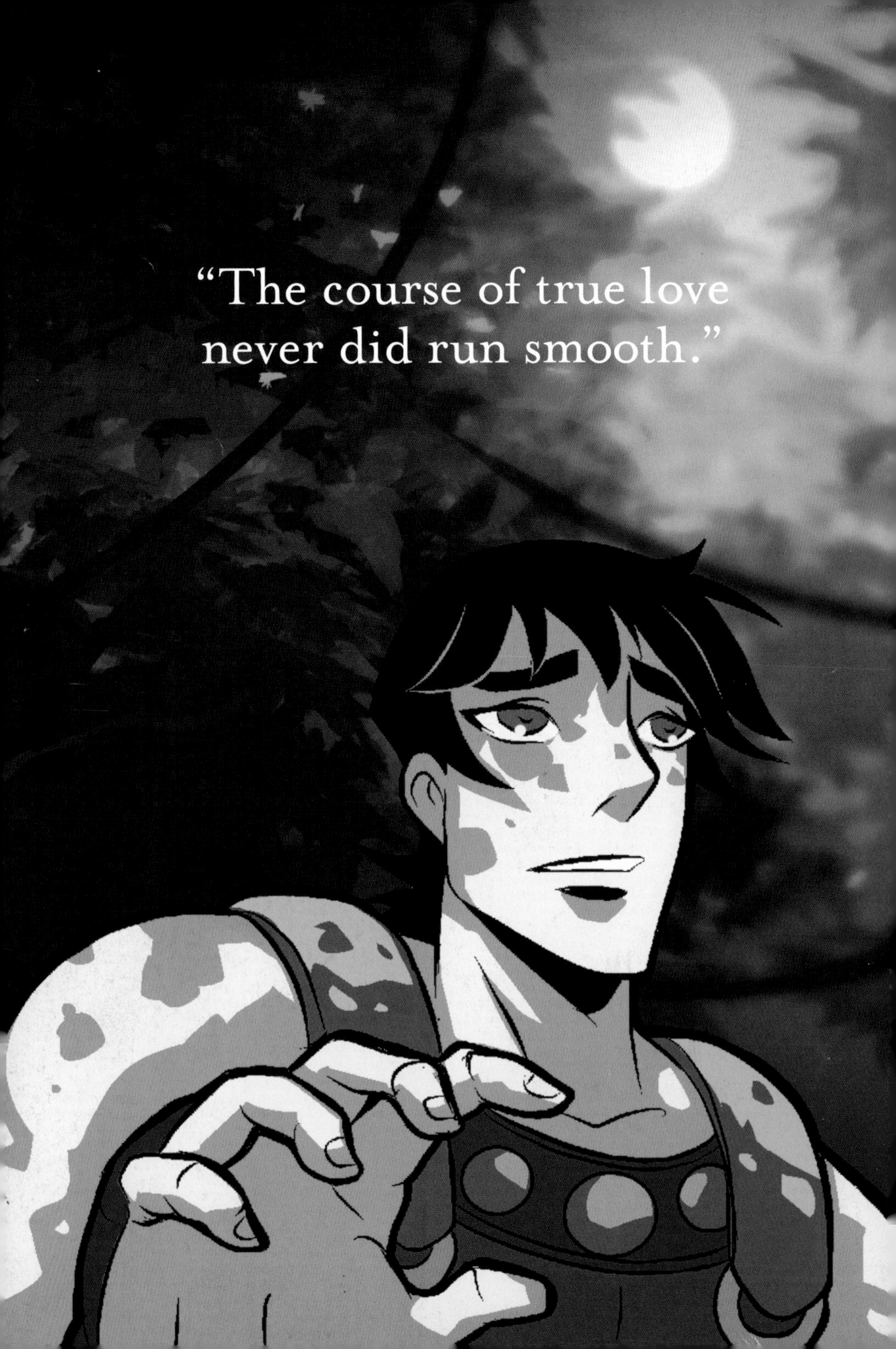
"The course of true love
never did run smooth."

ACT ONE

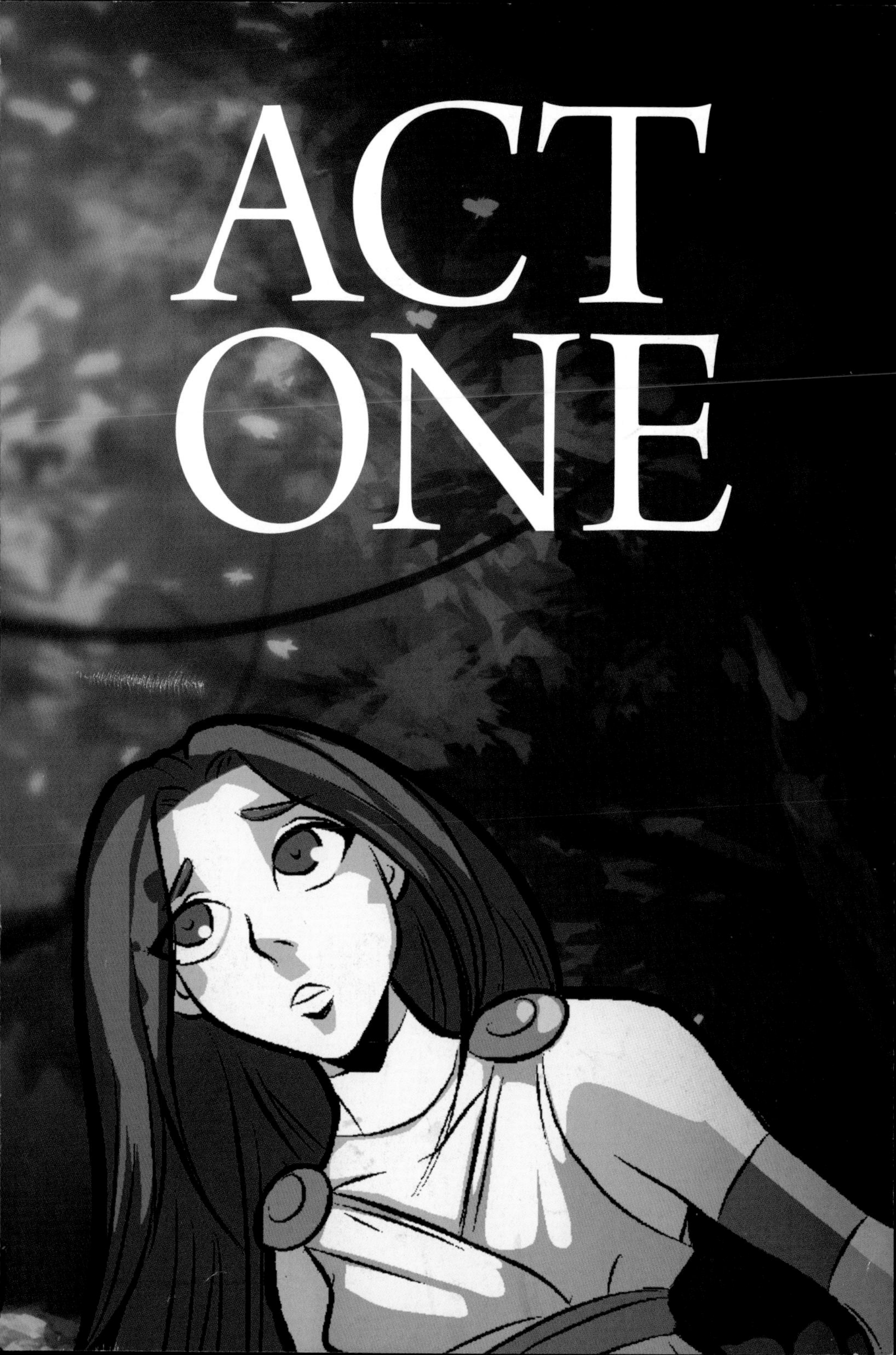

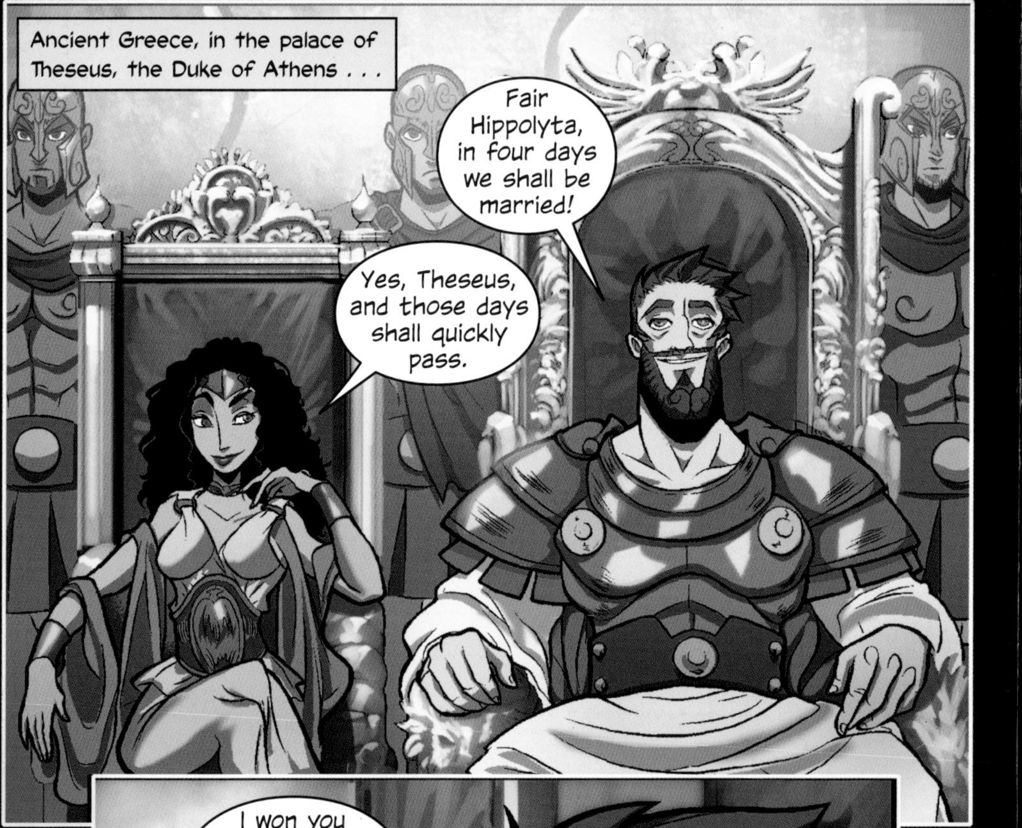
Ancient Greece, in the palace of Theseus, the Duke of Athens . . .
Fair Hippolyta, in four days we shall be married!
Yes, Theseus, and those days shall quickly pass.

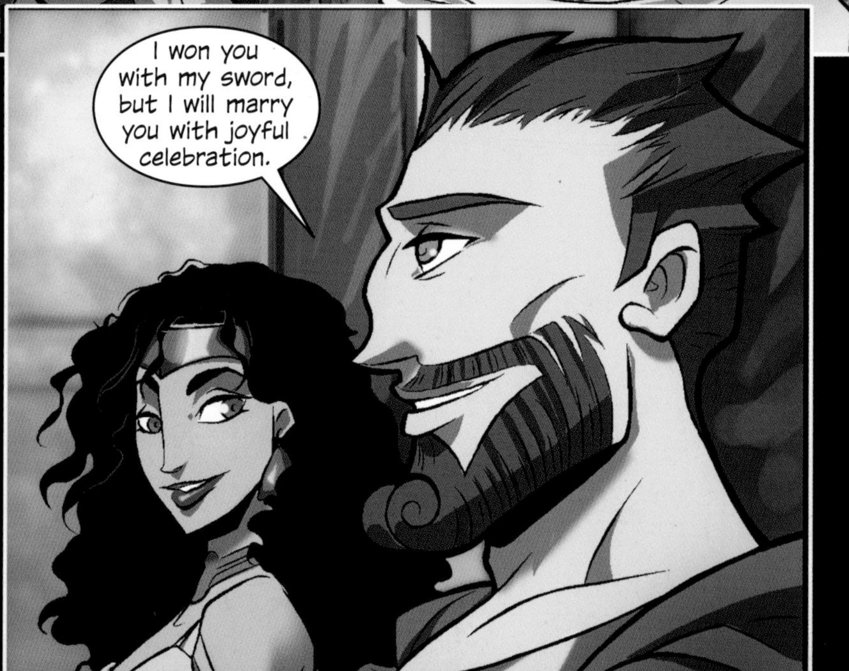
I won you with my sword, but I will marry you with joyful celebration.

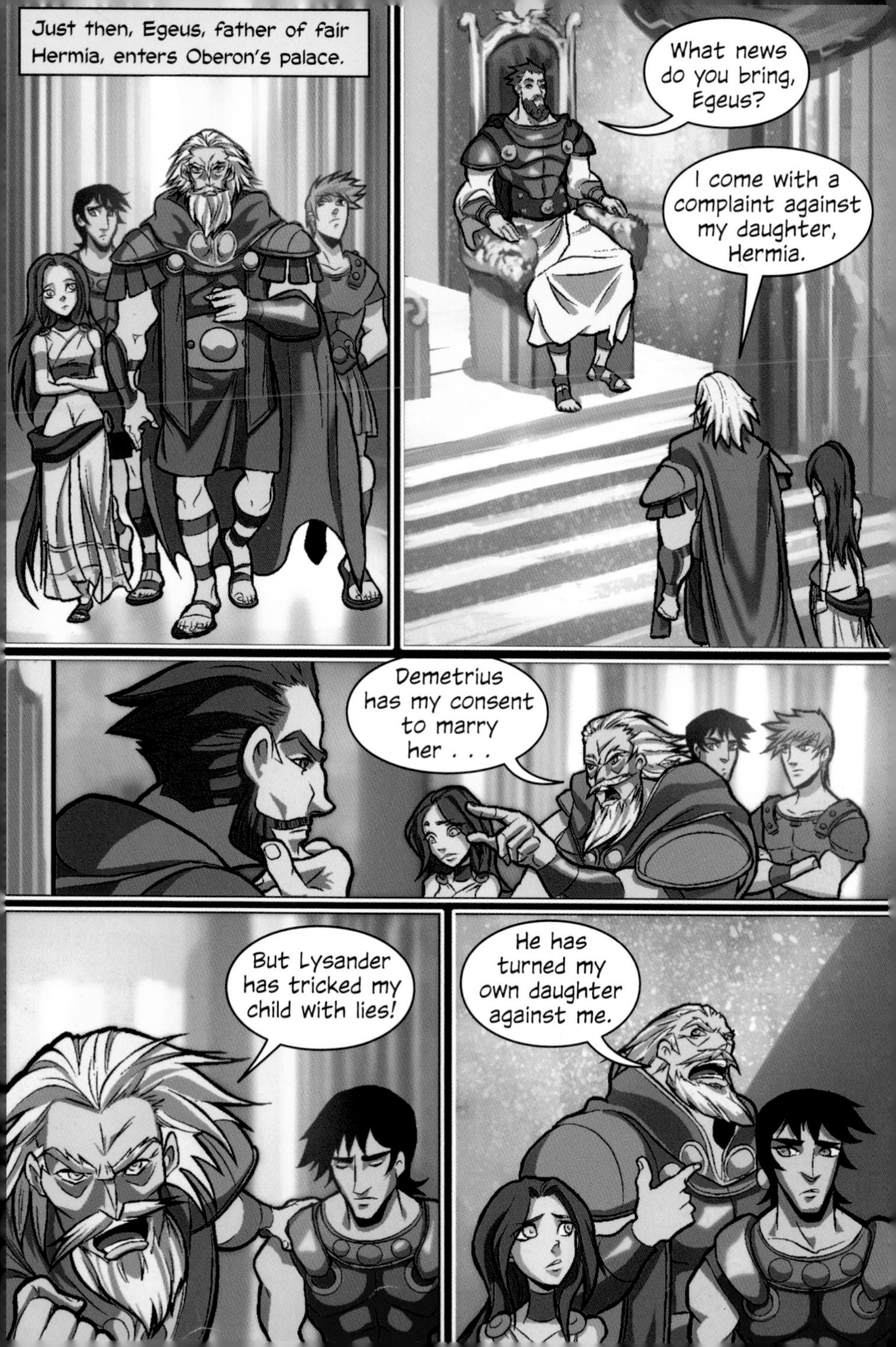
Just then, Egeus, father of fair Hermia, enters Oberon's palace.
What news do you bring, Egeus?
I come with a complaint against my daughter, Hermia.
Demetrius has my consent to marry her . . .
But Lysander has tricked my child with lies!
He has turned my own daughter against me.

I beg the ancient law of Athens that states . . .

. . . Lysander must be put to death!

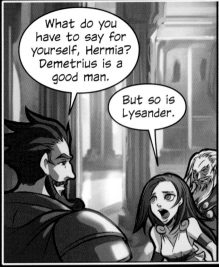

What do you have to say for yourself, Hermia? Demetrius is a good man.

But so is Lysander.

You should listen to your father, Hermia.

What is the worst that will happen to me if I refuse to marry Demetrius?

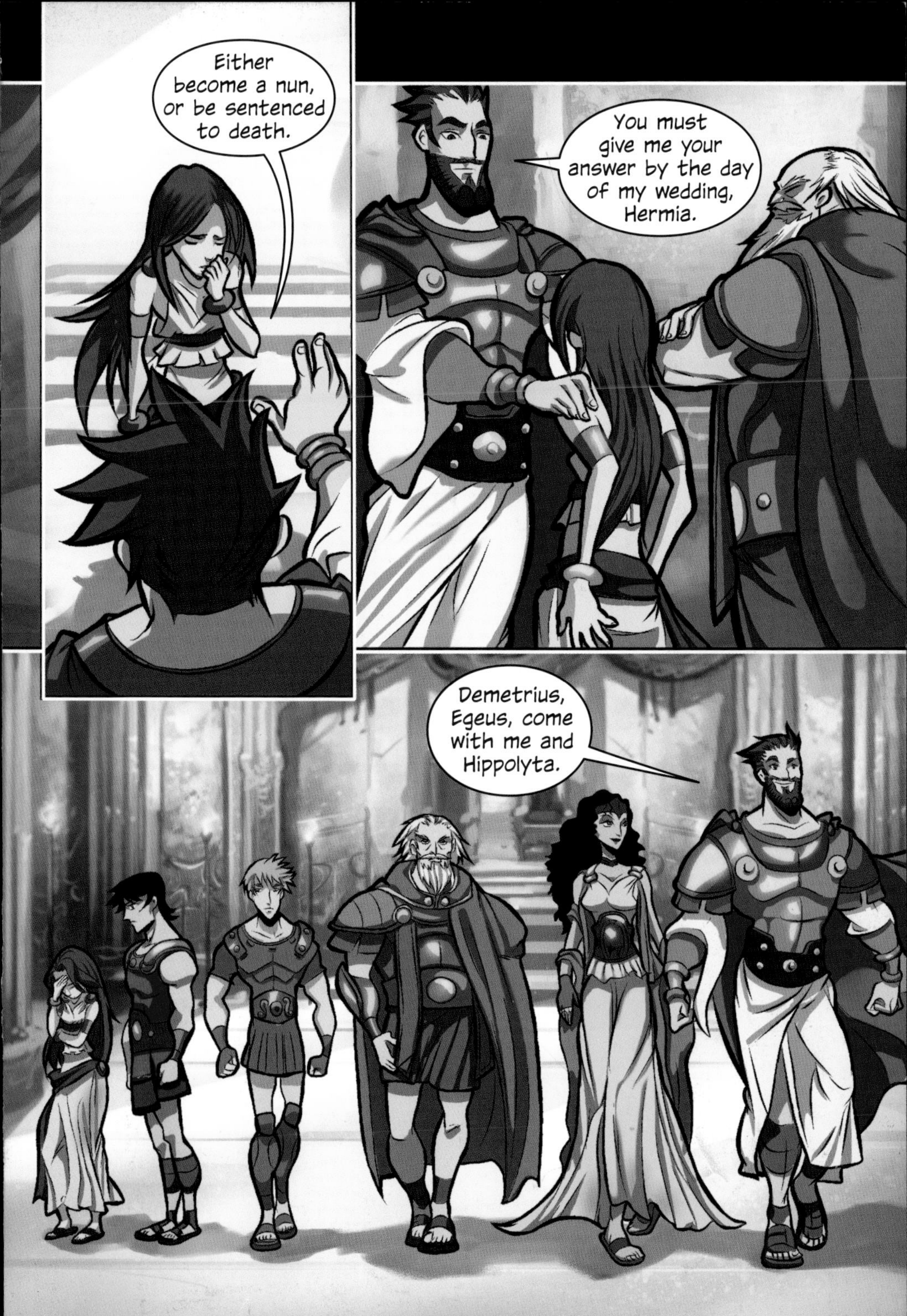
Either become a nun, or be sentenced to death.
You must give me your answer by the day of my wedding, Hermia.
Demetrius, Egeus, come with me and Hippolyta.

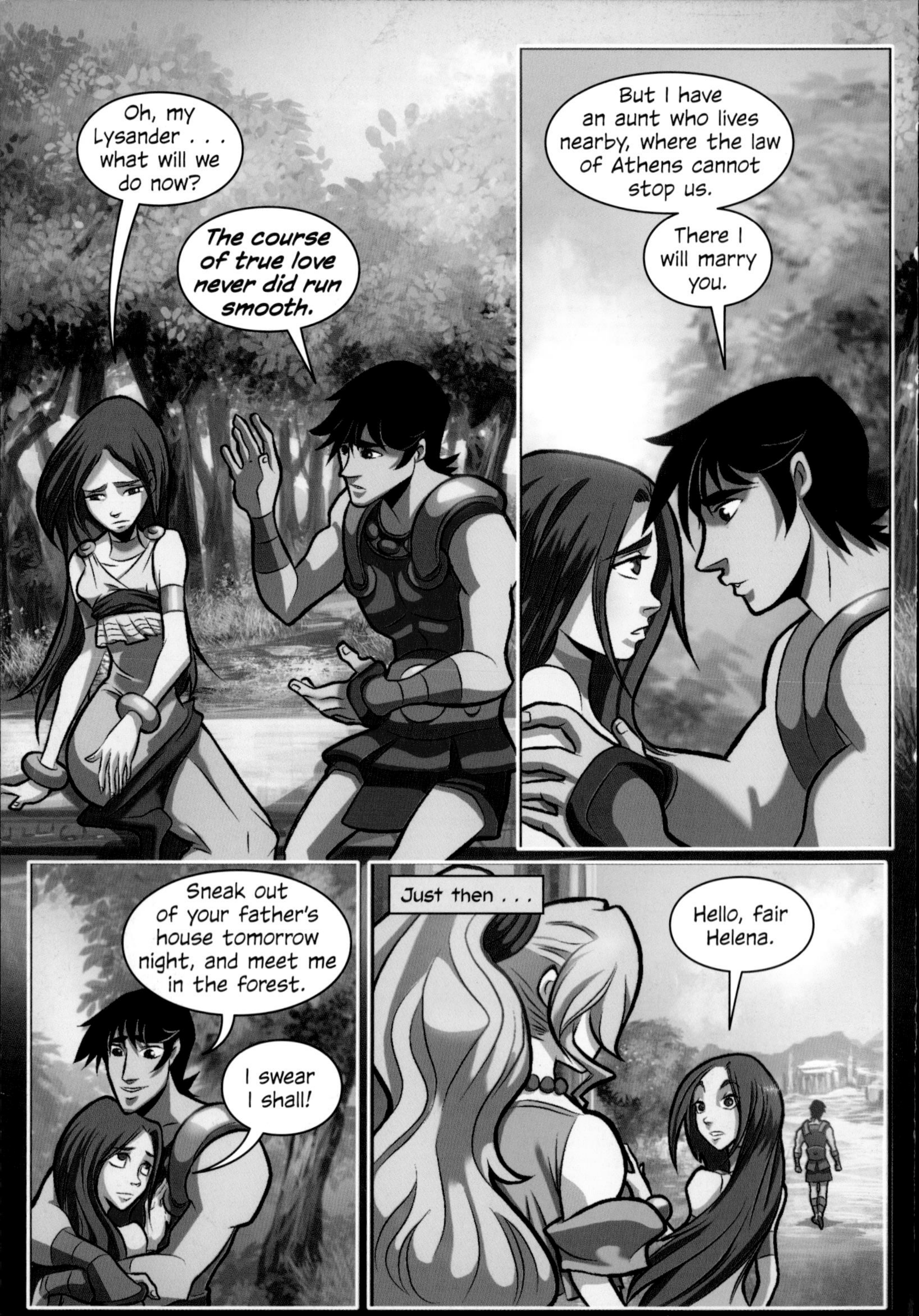
Oh, my Lysander . . . what will we do now?
The course of true love never did run smooth.
But I have an aunt who lives nearby, where the law of Athens cannot stop us.
There I will marry you.
Sneak out of your father's house tomorrow night, and meet me in the forest.
I swear I shall!
Just then . . .
Hello, fair Helena.

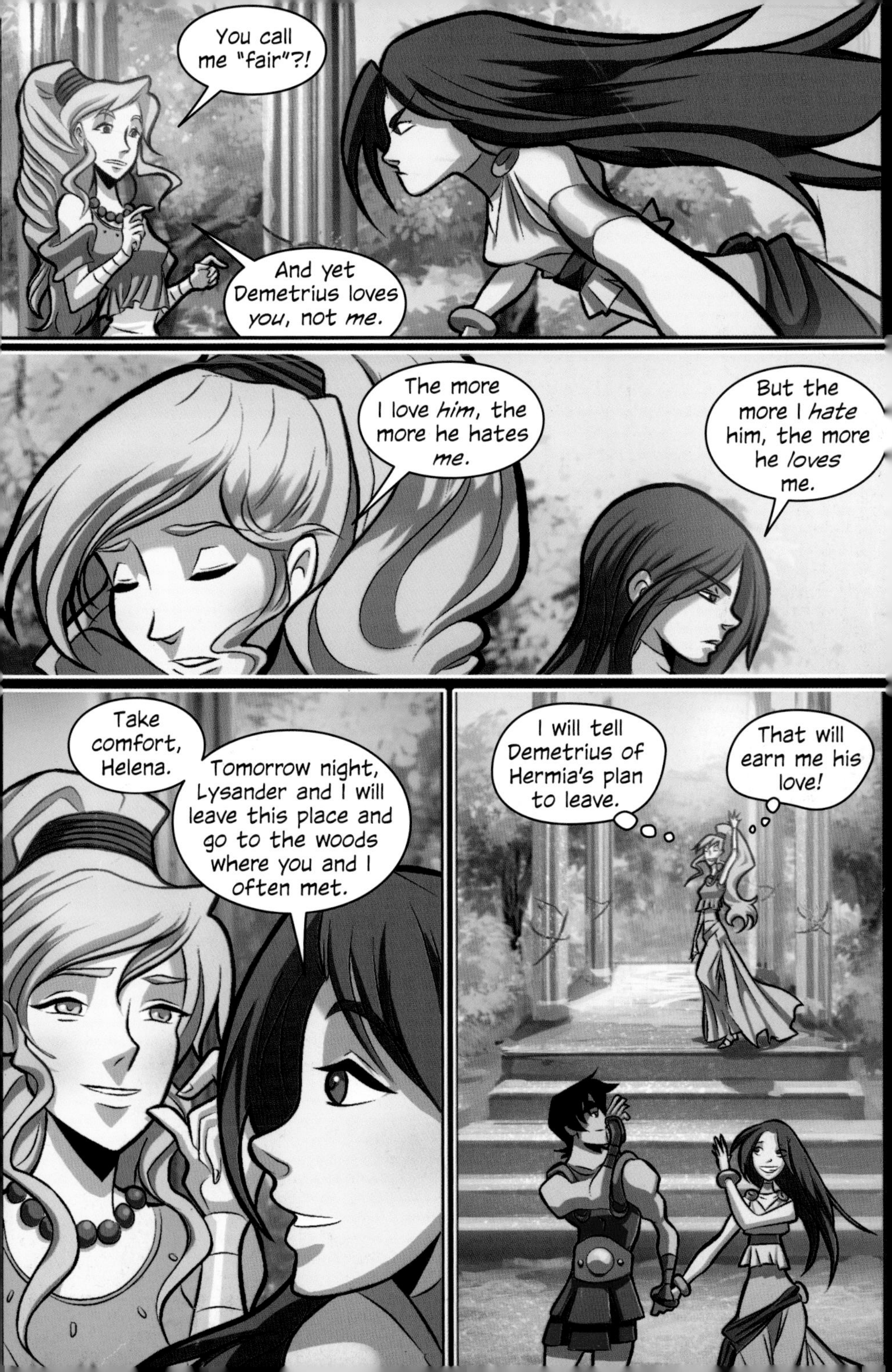
You call me "fair"?!
And yet Demetrius loves *you*, not *me*.
The more I love *him*, the more he hates *me*.
But the more I *hate* him, the more he *loves* me.
Take comfort, Helena.
Tomorrow night, Lysander and I will leave this place and go to the woods where you and I often met.
I will tell Demetrius of Hermia's plan to leave.
That will earn me his love!

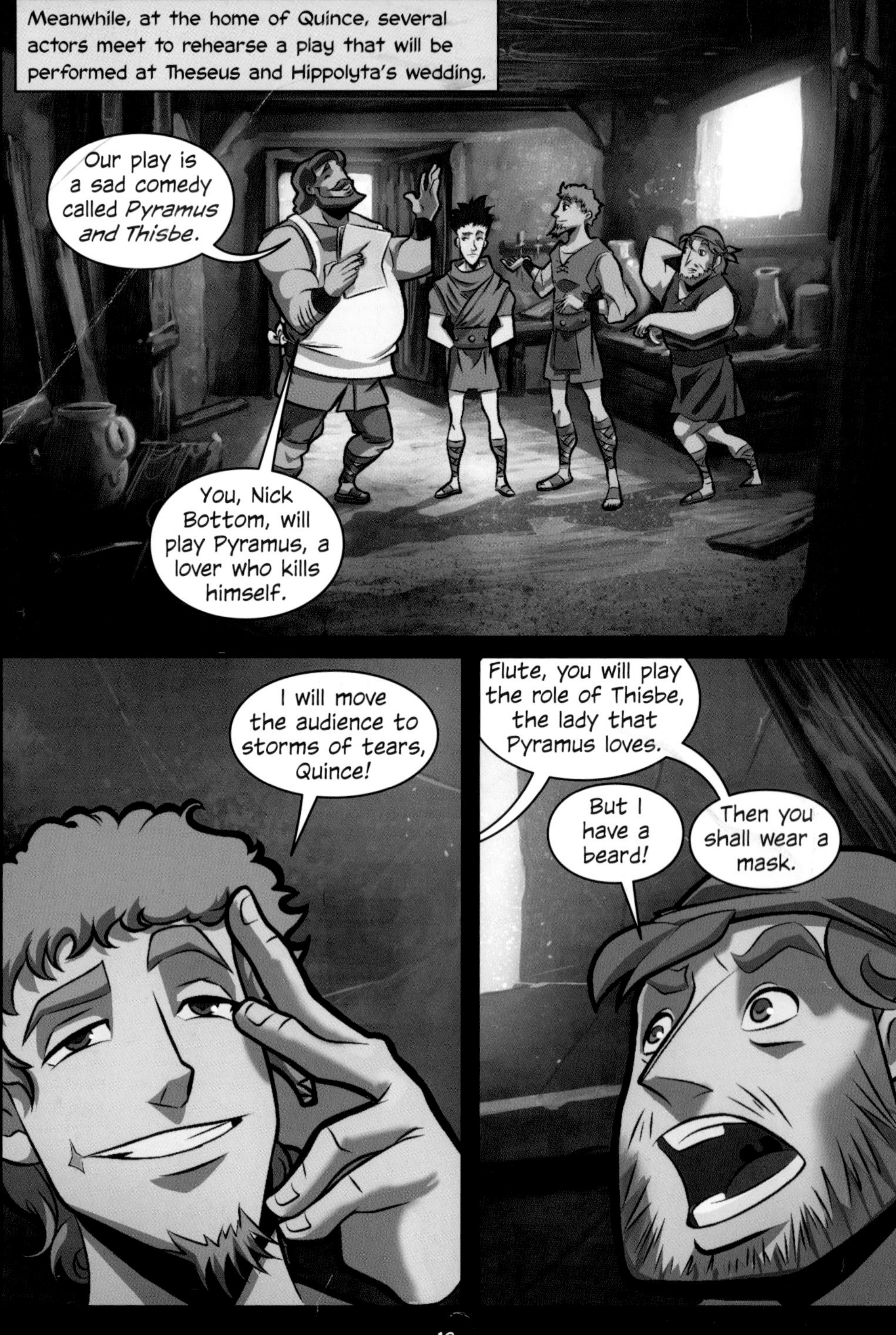
Meanwhile, at the home of Quince, several actors meet to rehearse a play that will be performed at Theseus and Hippolyta's wedding.
Our play is a sad comedy called *Pyramus and Thisbe.*
You, Nick Bottom, will play Pyramus, a lover who kills himself.
I will move the audience to storms of tears, Quince!
Flute, you will play the role of Thisbe, the lady that Pyramus loves.
But I have a beard!
Then you shall wear a mask.

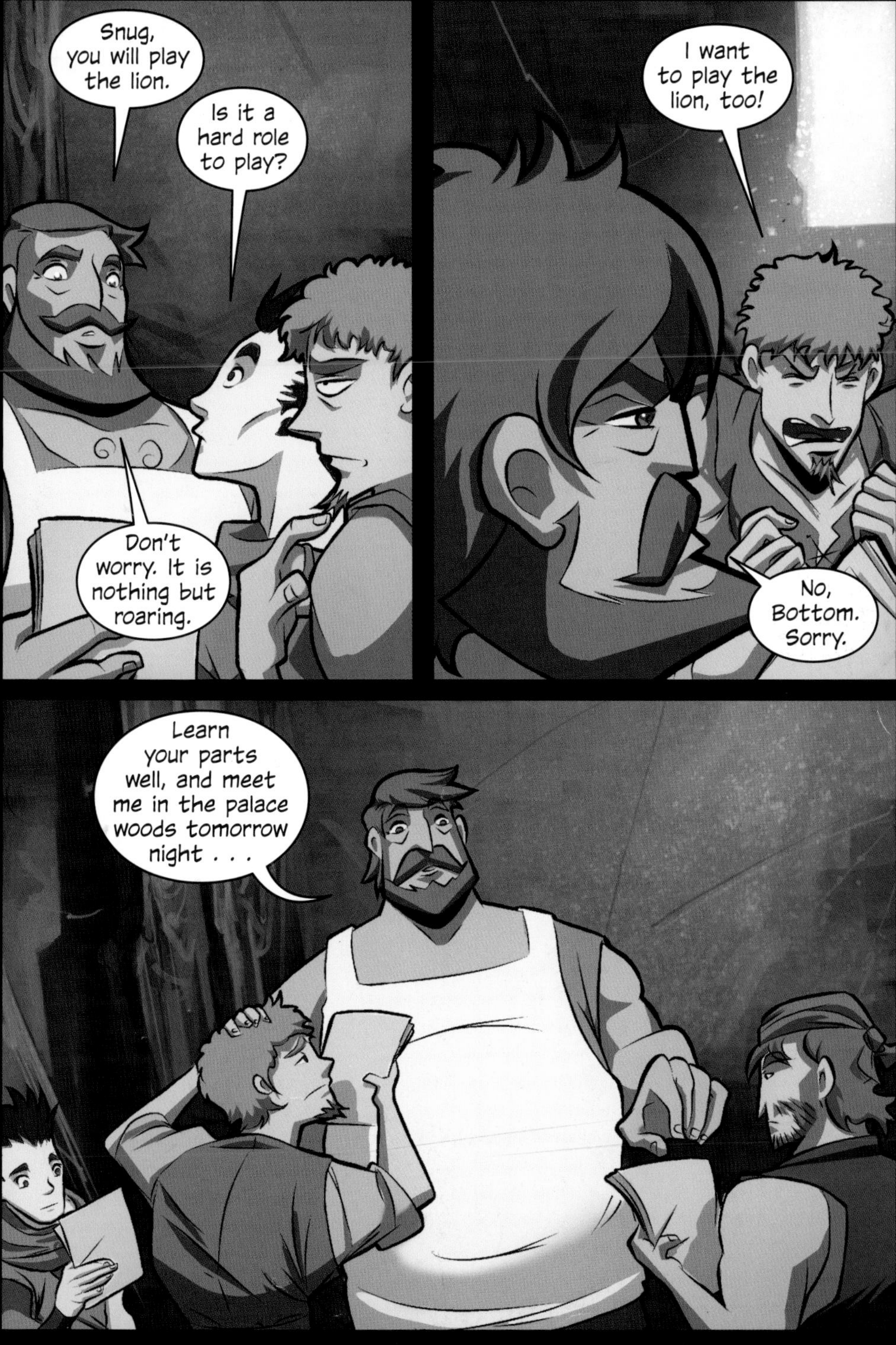
Snug, you will play the lion.
Is it a hard role to play?
Don't worry. It is nothing but roaring.
I want to play the lion, too!
No, Bottom. Sorry.
Learn your parts well, and meet me in the palace woods tomorrow night . . .

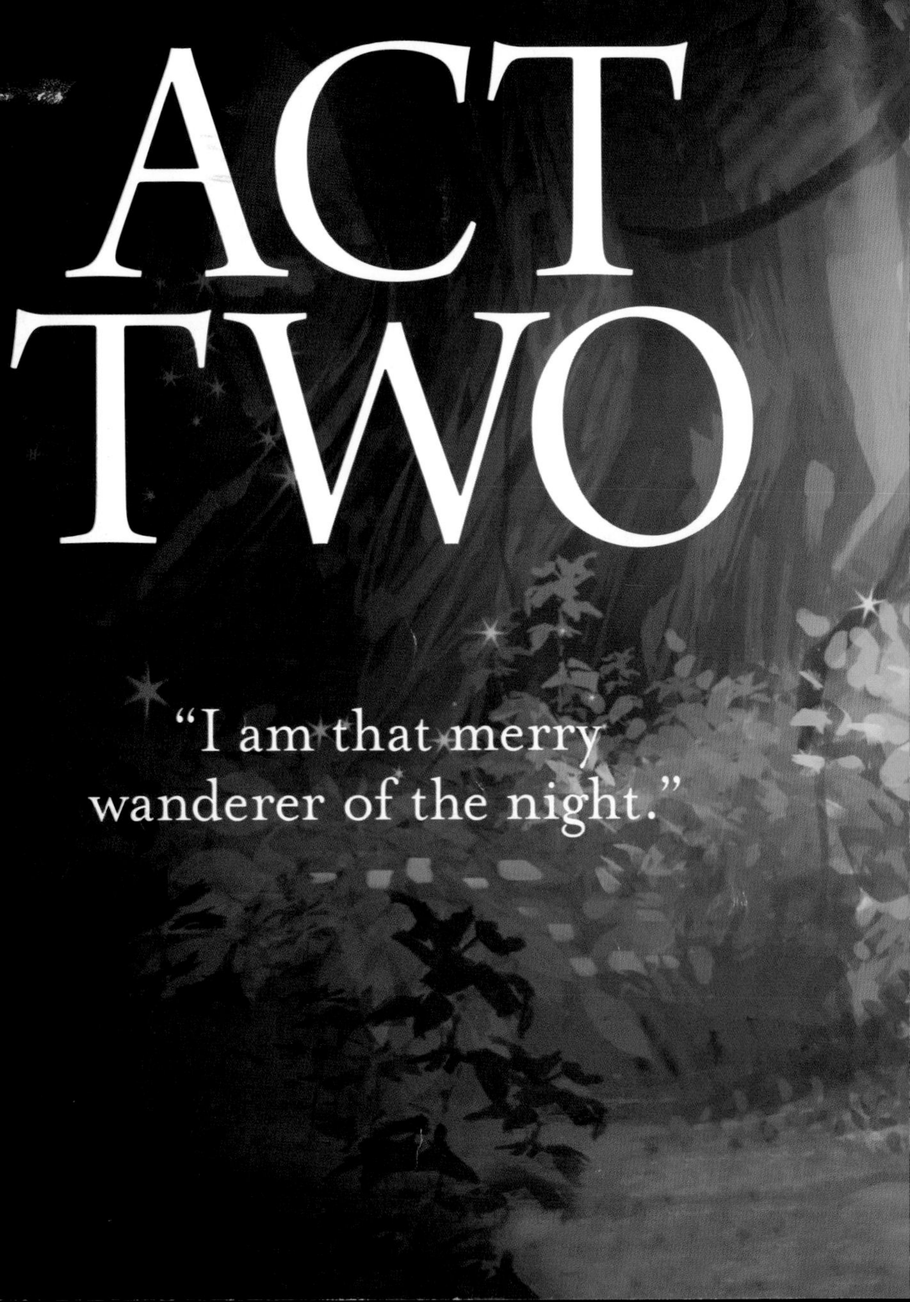

ACT TWO

"I am that merry wanderer of the night."

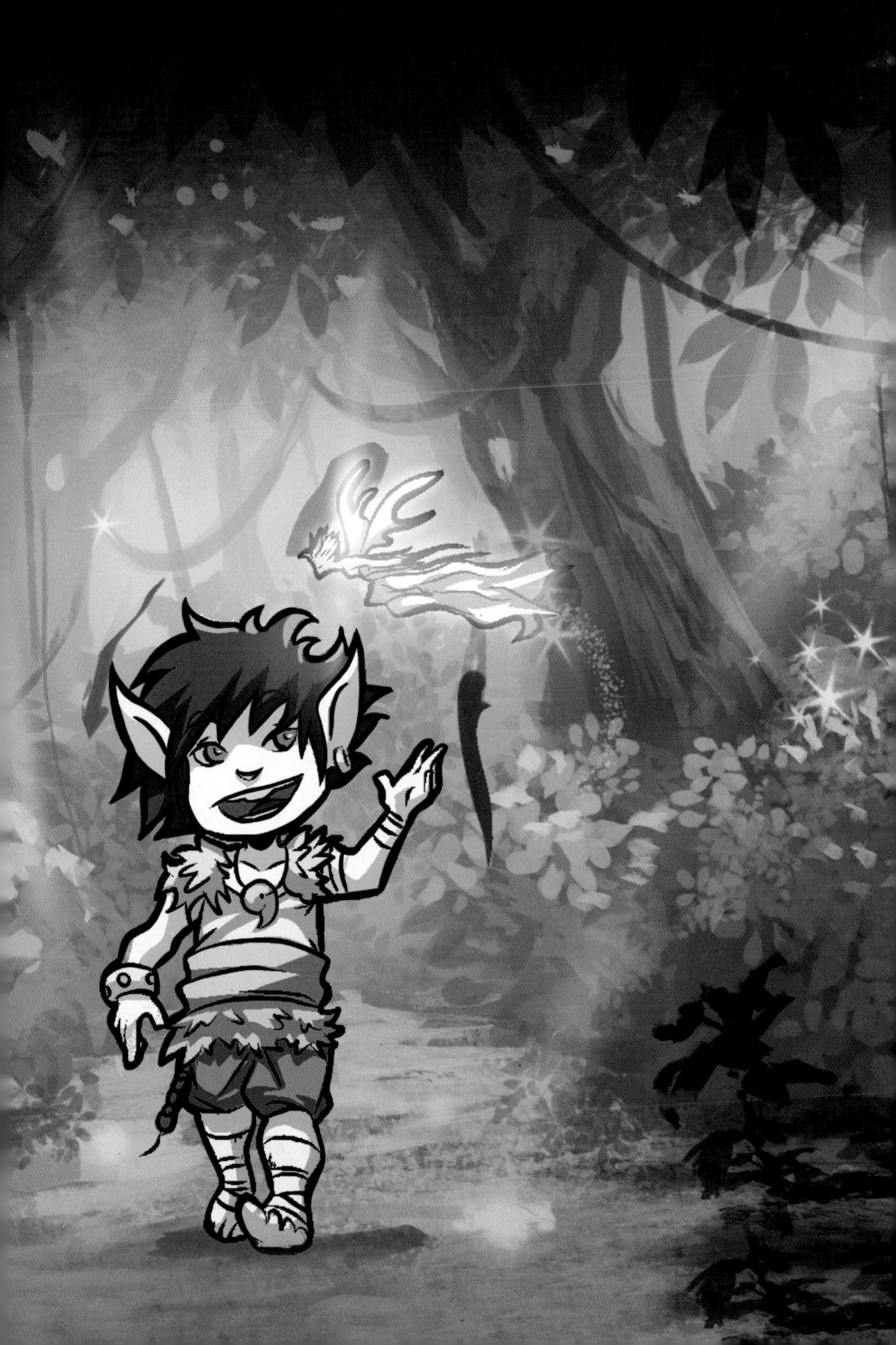

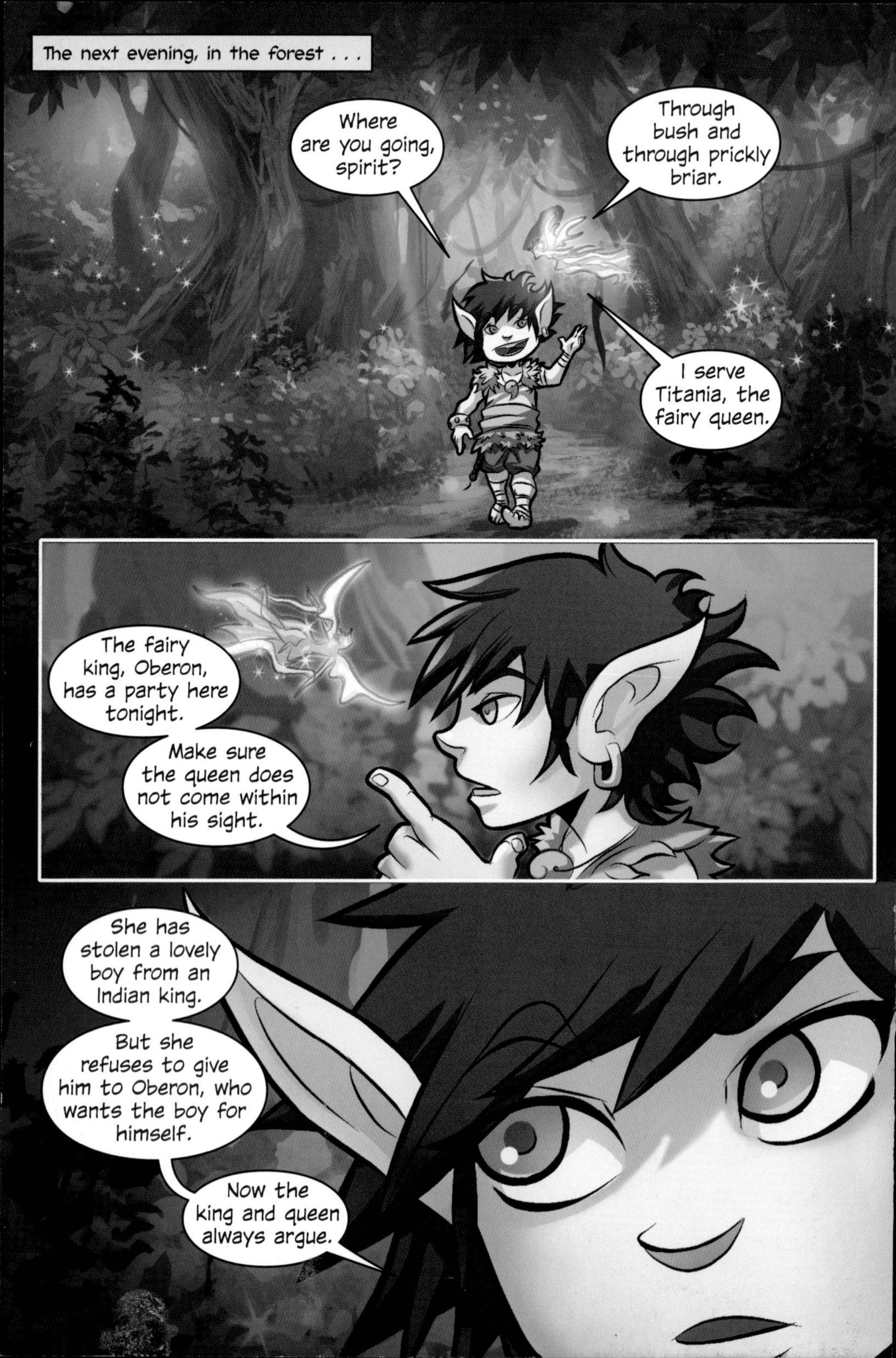
The next evening, in the forest . . .
Where are you going, spirit?
Through bush and through prickly briar.
I serve Titania, the fairy queen.
The fairy king, Oberon, has a party here tonight.
Make sure the queen does not come within his sight.
She has stolen a lovely boy from an Indian king.
But she refuses to give him to Oberon, who wants the boy for himself.
Now the king and queen always argue.

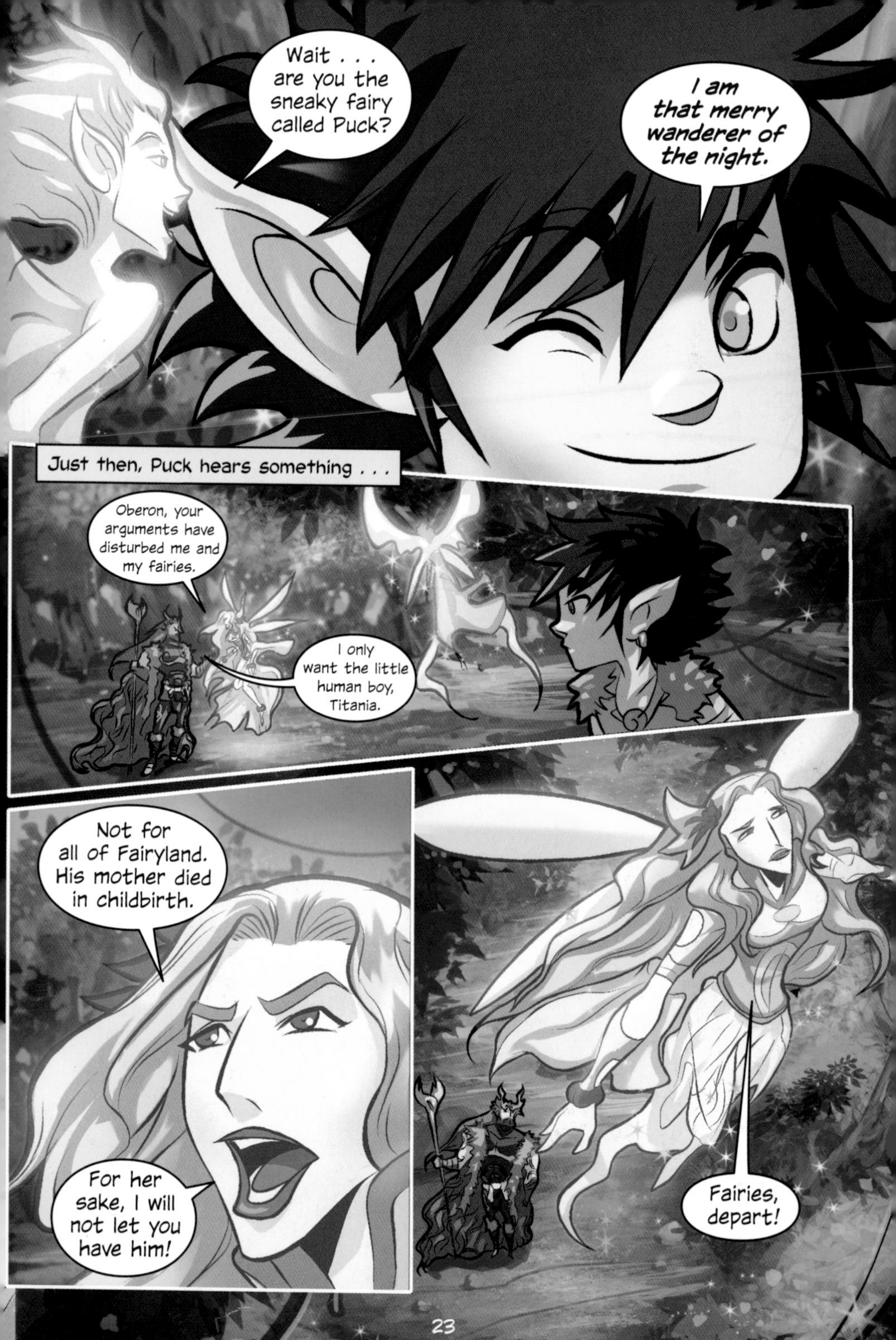
Wait . . . are you the sneaky fairy called Puck?
I am that merry wanderer of the night.
Just then, Puck hears something . . .
Oberon, your arguments have disturbed me and my fairies.
I only want the little human boy, Titania.
Not for all of Fairyland. His mother died in childbirth.
For her sake, I will not let you have him!
Fairies, depart!

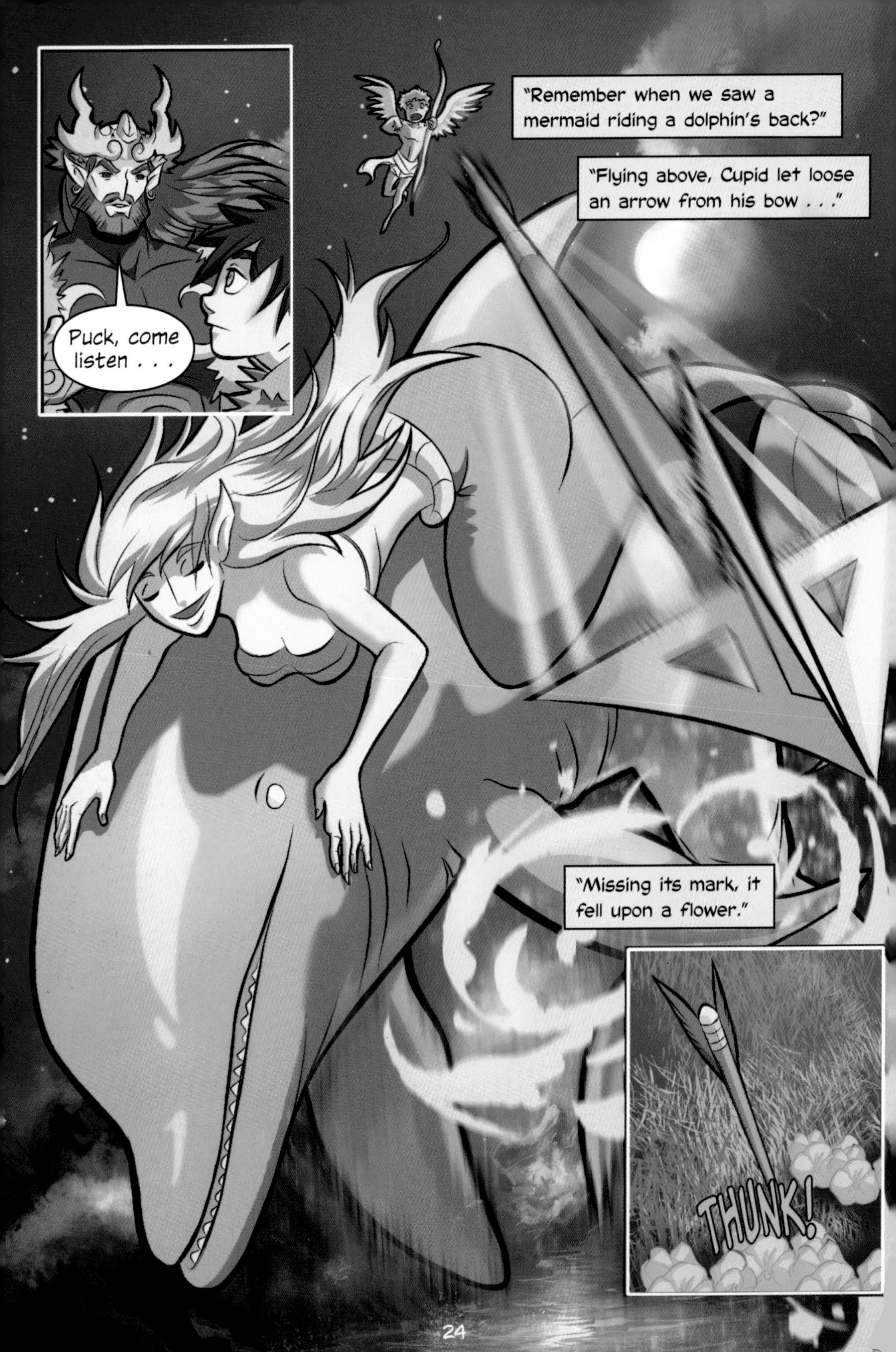
Puck, come listen . . .
"Remember when we saw a mermaid riding a dolphin's back?"
"Flying above, Cupid let loose an arrow from his bow . . ."
"Missing its mark, it fell upon a flower."
THUNK!

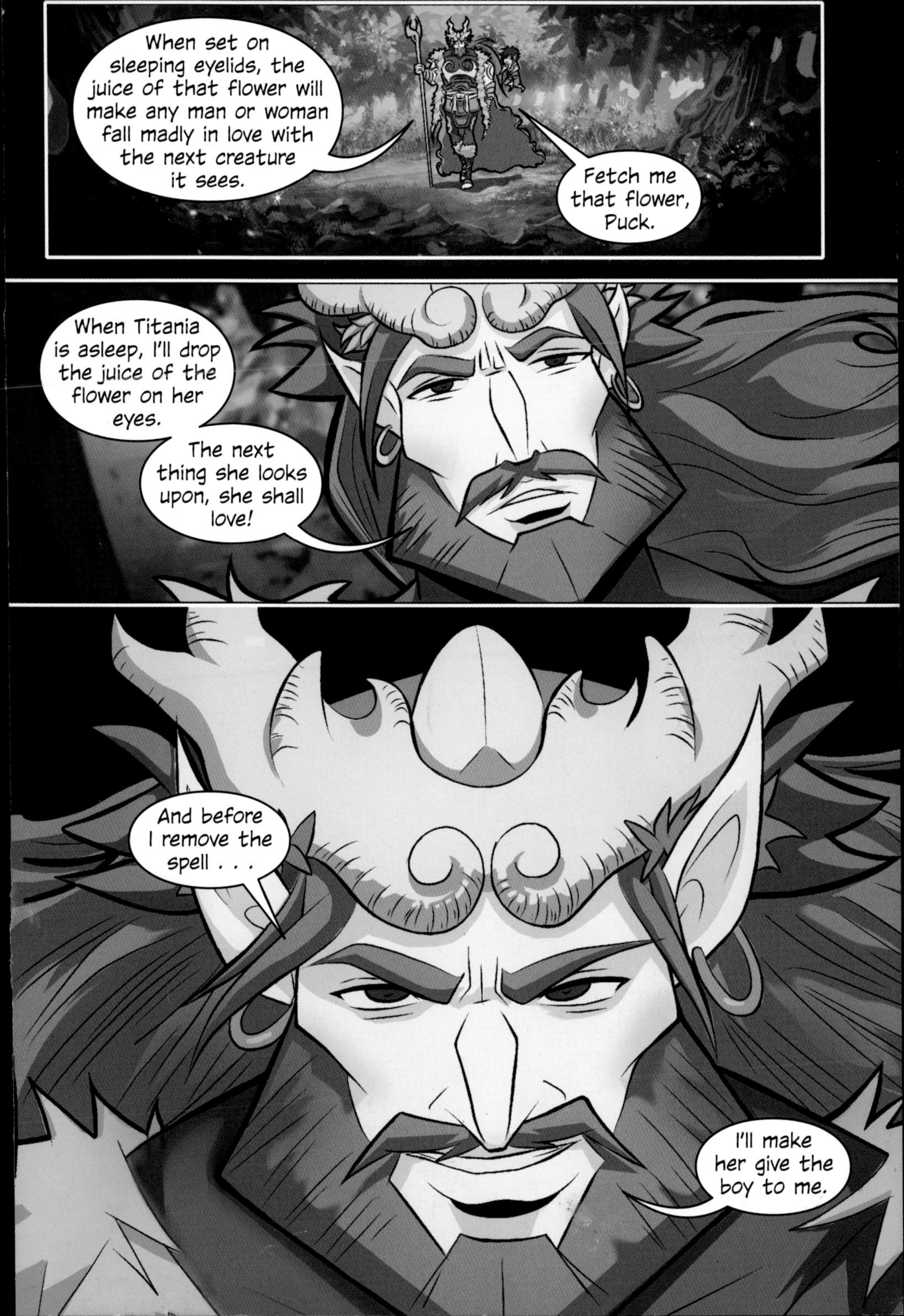
When set on sleeping eyelids, the juice of that flower will make any man or woman fall madly in love with the next creature it sees.
Fetch me that flower, Puck.
When Titania is asleep, I'll drop the juice of the flower on her eyes.
The next thing she looks upon, she shall love!
And before I remove the spell . . .
I'll make her give the boy to me.

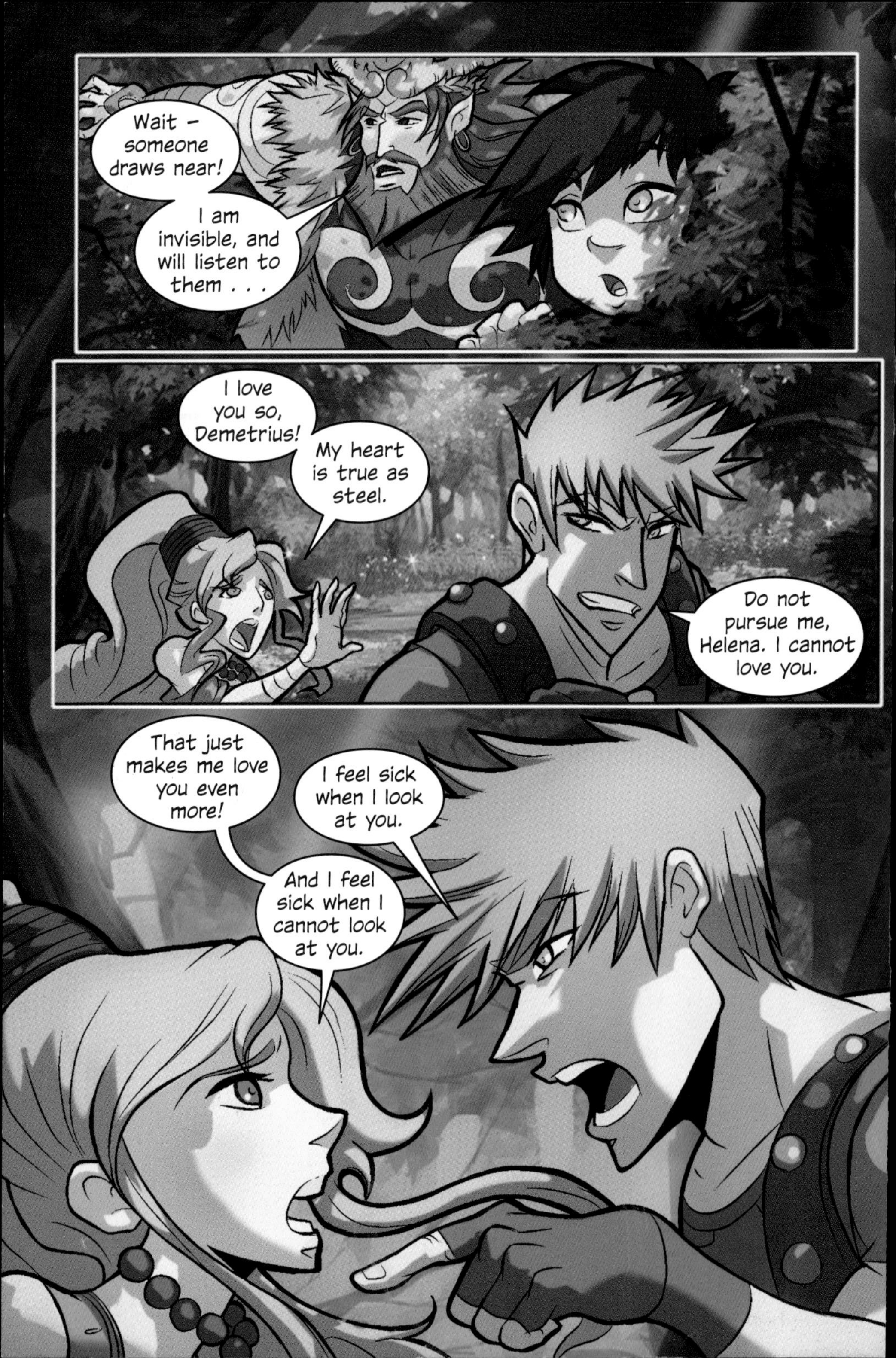
Wait – someone draws near!
I am invisible, and will listen to them . . .
I love you so, Demetrius!
My heart is true as steel.
Do not pursue me, Helena. I cannot love you.
That just makes me love you even more!
I feel sick when I look at you.
And I feel sick when I cannot look at you.

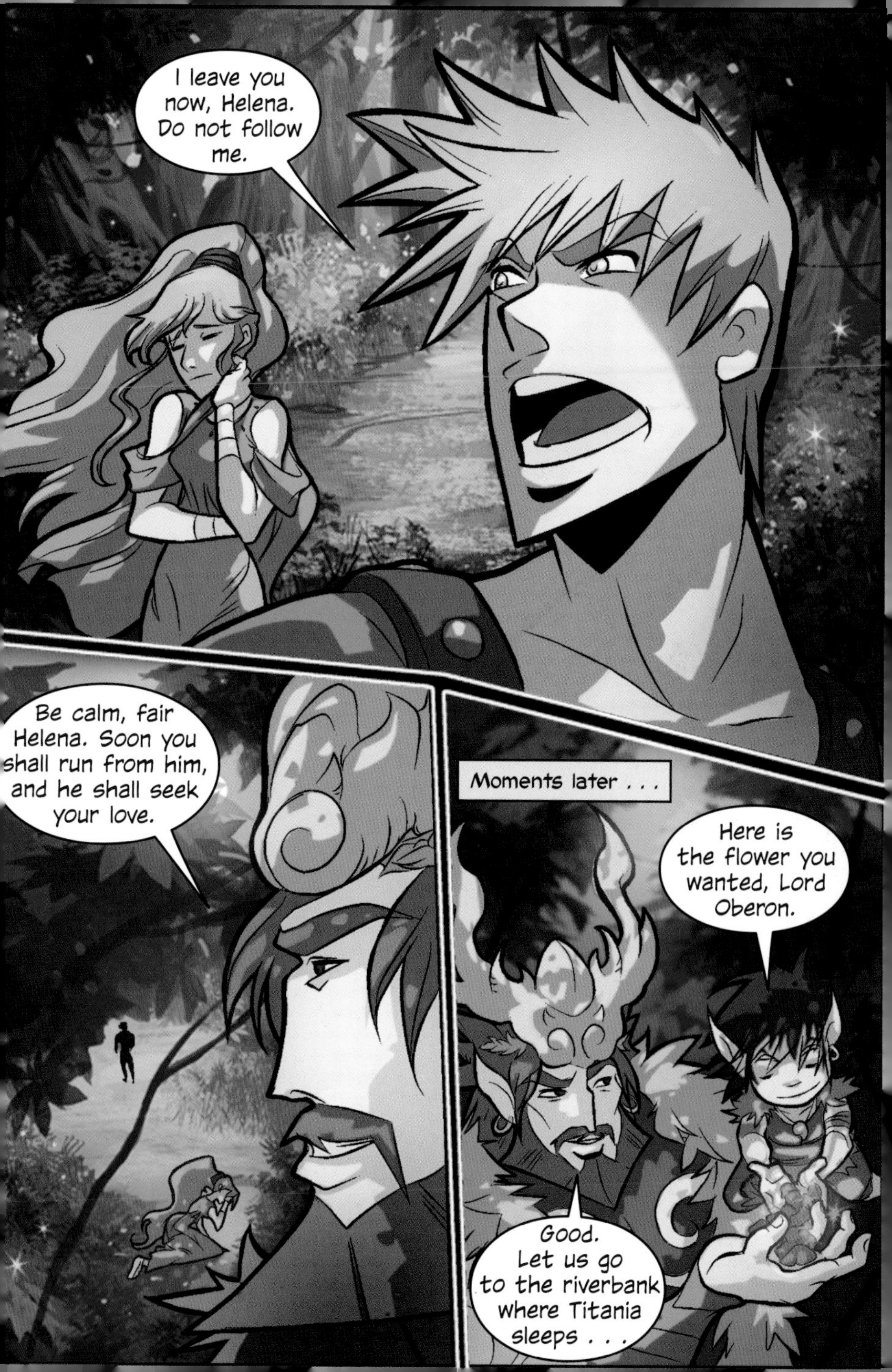
I leave you now, Helena. Do not follow me.
Be calm, fair Helena. Soon you shall run from him, and he shall seek your love.
Moments later . . .
Here is the flower you wanted, Lord Oberon.
Good. Let us go to the riverbank where Titania sleeps . . .

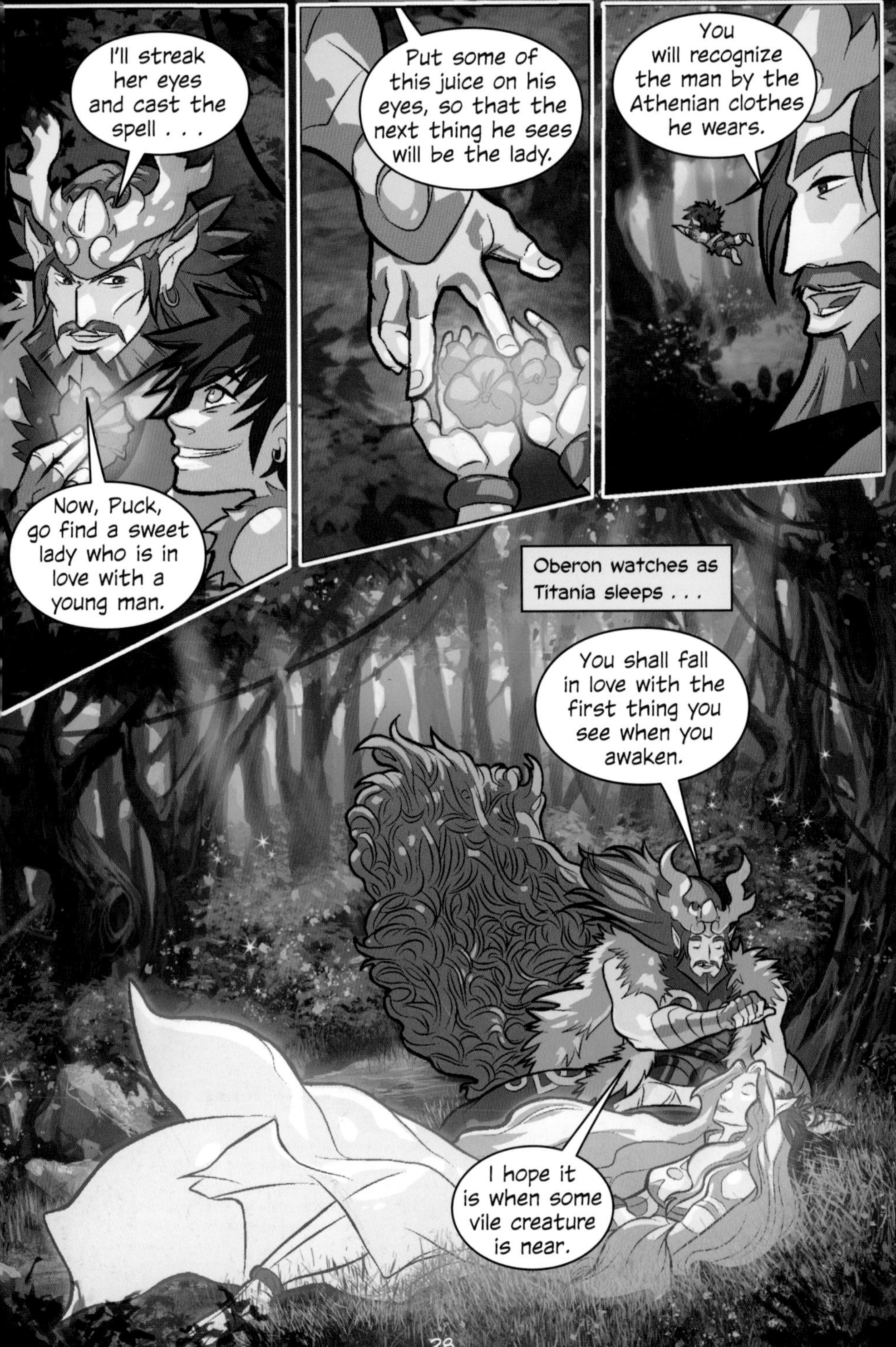
I'll streak her eyes and cast the spell . . .
Now, Puck, go find a sweet lady who is in love with a young man.
Put some of this juice on his eyes, so that the next thing he sees will be the lady.
You will recognize the man by the Athenian clothes he wears.
Oberon watches as Titania sleeps . . .
You shall fall in love with the first thing you see when you awaken.
I hope it is when some vile creature is near.

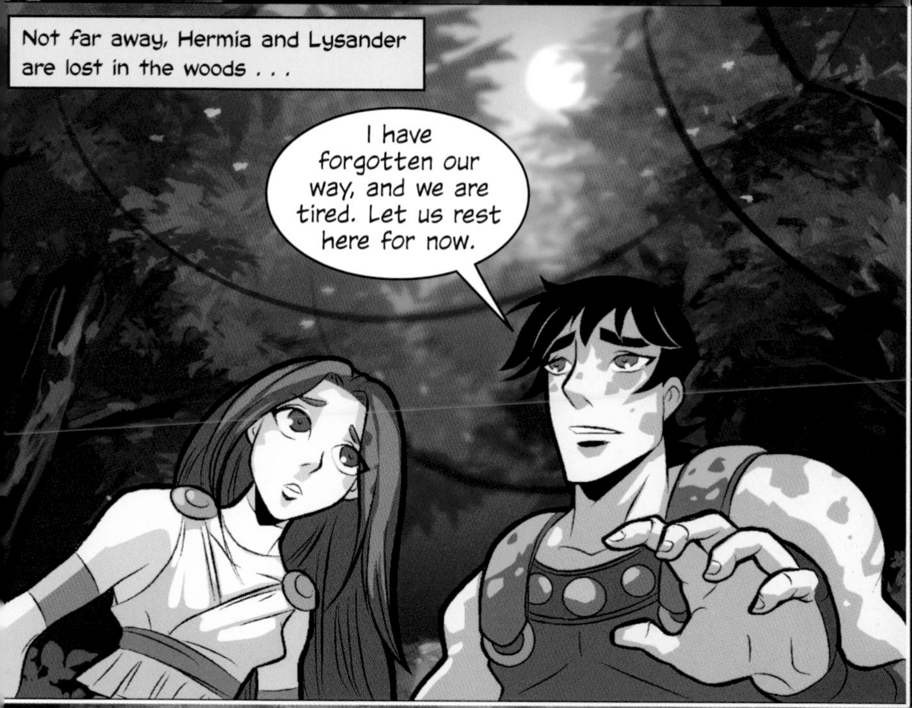
Not far away, Hermia and Lysander are lost in the woods . . .
I have forgotten our way, and we are tired. Let us rest here for now.
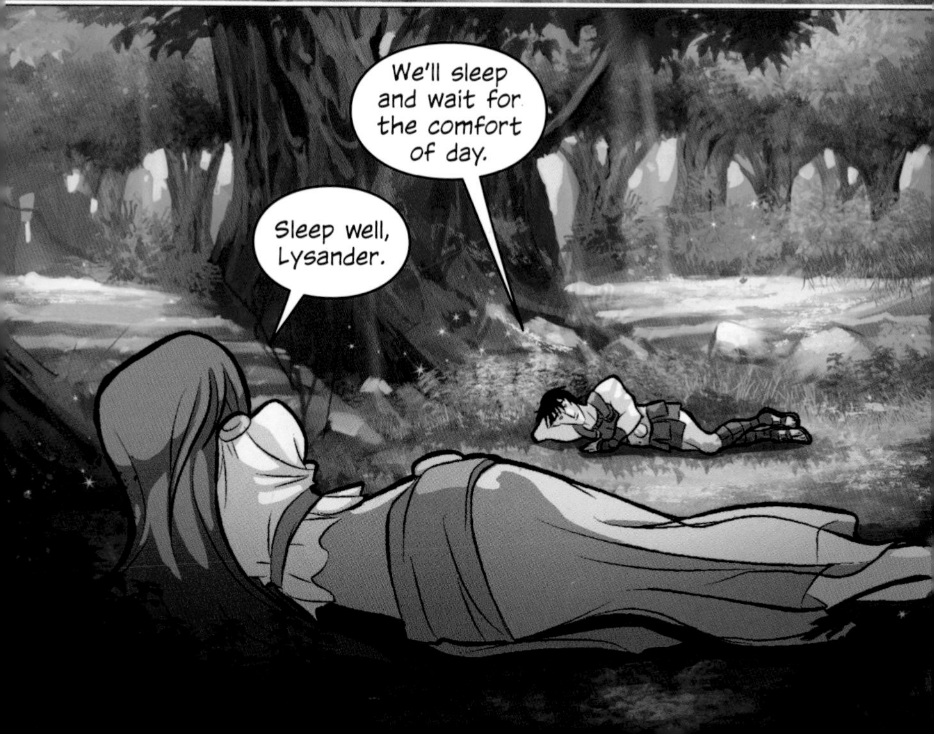
We'll sleep and wait for the comfort of day.
Sleep well, Lysander.

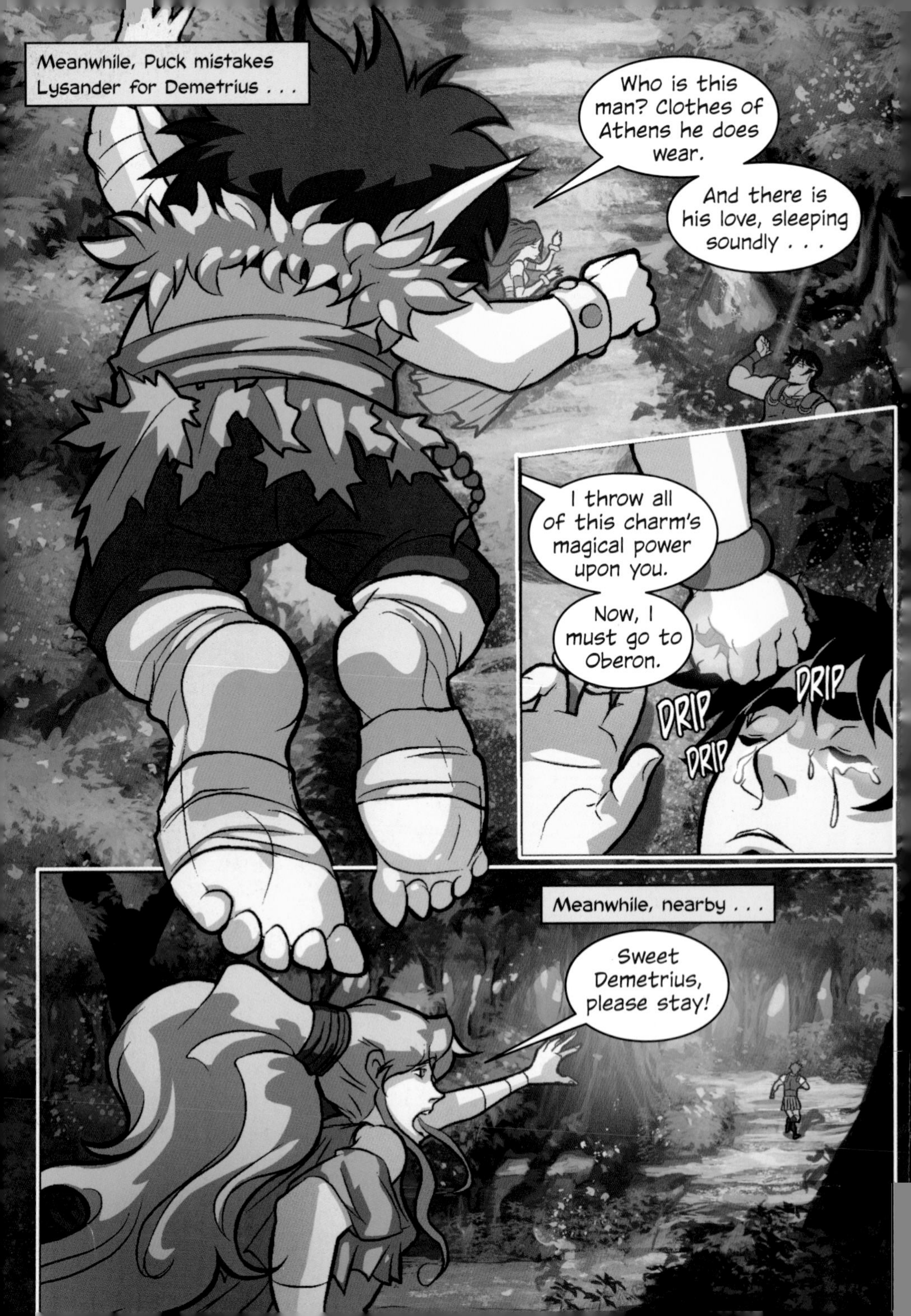
Meanwhile, Puck mistakes Lysander for Demetrius . . .
Who is this man? Clothes of Athens he does wear.
And there is his love, sleeping soundly . . .
I throw all of this charm's magical power upon you.
Now, I must go to Oberon.
DRIP
DRIP
DRIP
Meanwhile, nearby . . .
Sweet Demetrius, please stay!

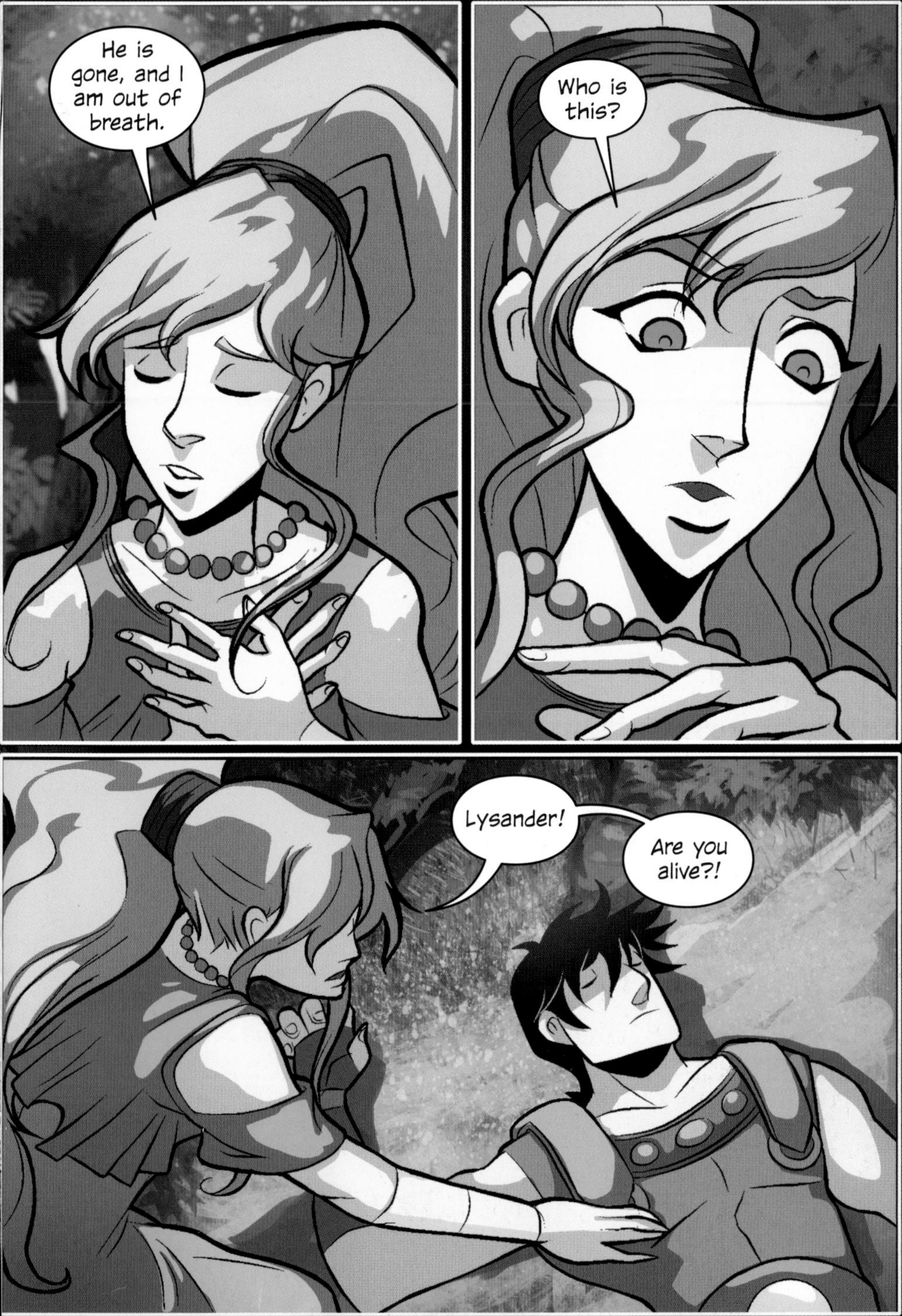
He is gone, and I am out of breath.
Who is this?
Lysander!
Are you alive?!

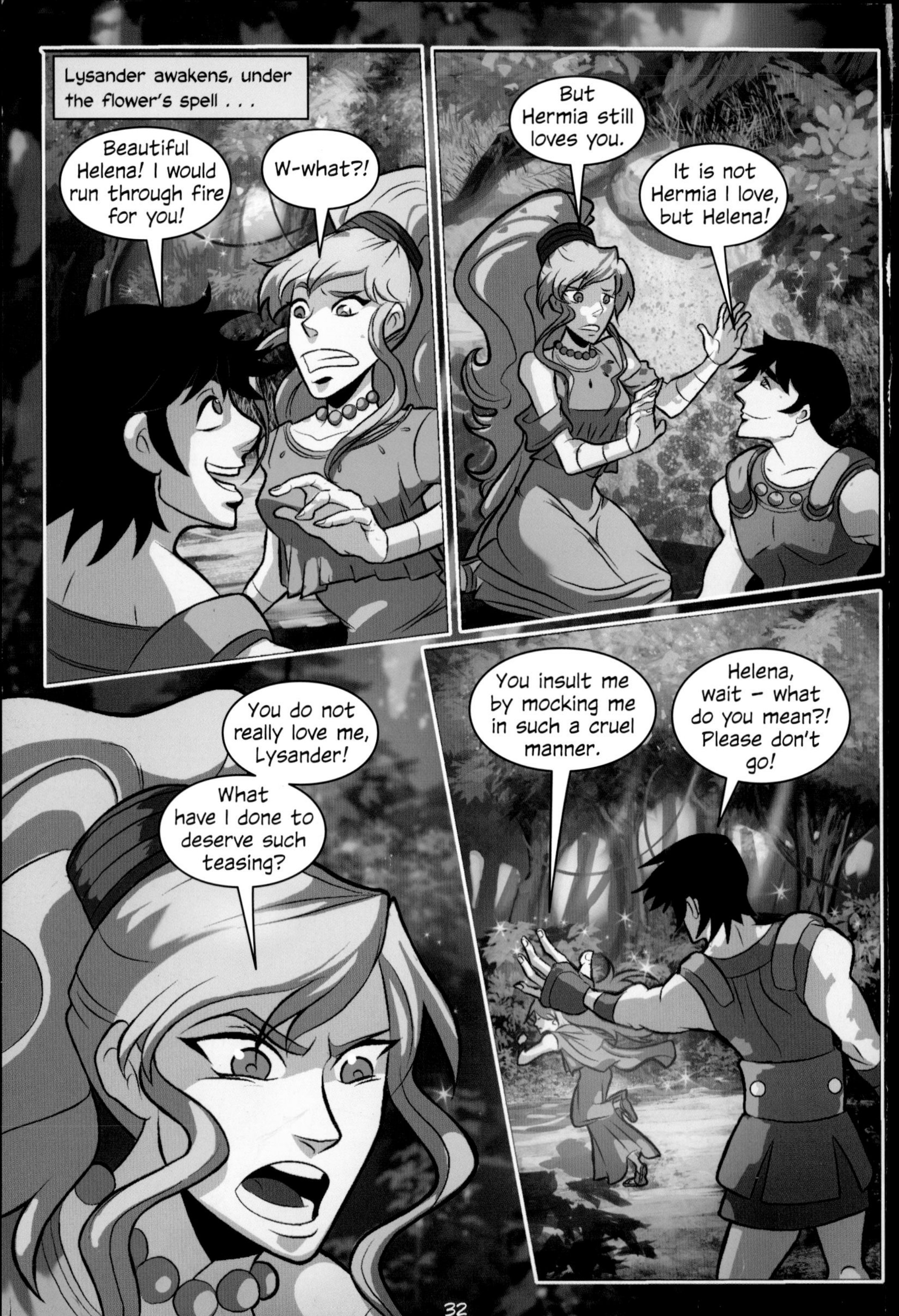
Lysander awakens, under the flower's spell . . .
Beautiful Helena! I would run through fire for you!
W-what?!
But Hermia still loves you.
It is not Hermia I love, but Helena!
You do not really love me, Lysander!
What have I done to deserve such teasing?
You insult me by mocking me in such a cruel manner.
Helena, wait – what do you mean?! Please don't go!

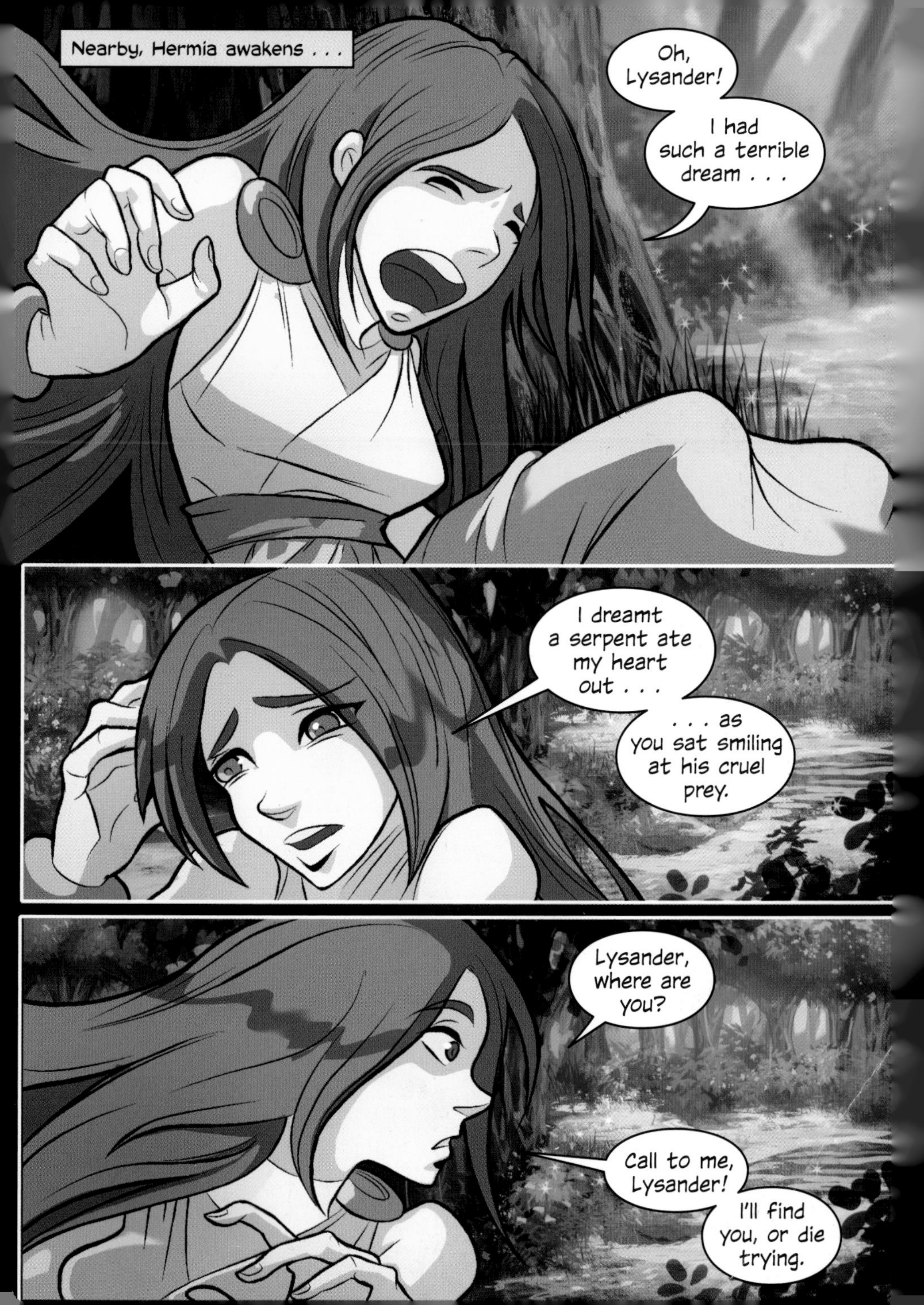

Nearby, Hermia awakens . . .
Oh, Lysander!
I had such a terrible dream . . .
I dreamt a serpent ate my heart out . . .
. . . as you sat smiling at his cruel prey.
Lysander, where are you?
Call to me, Lysander!
I'll find you, or die trying.

"And yet, to say the truth, reason and love keep little company together nowadays."

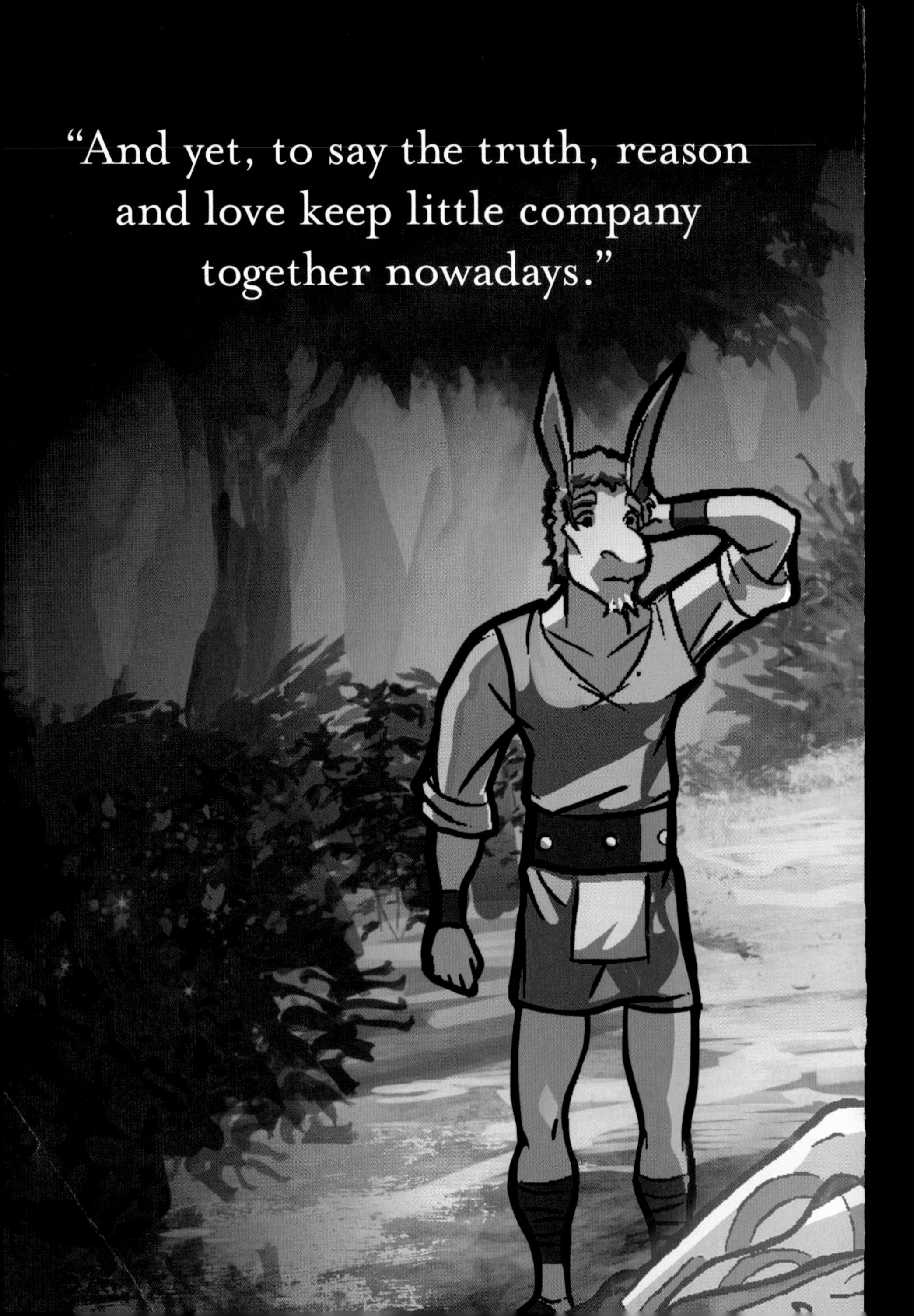

ACT THREE

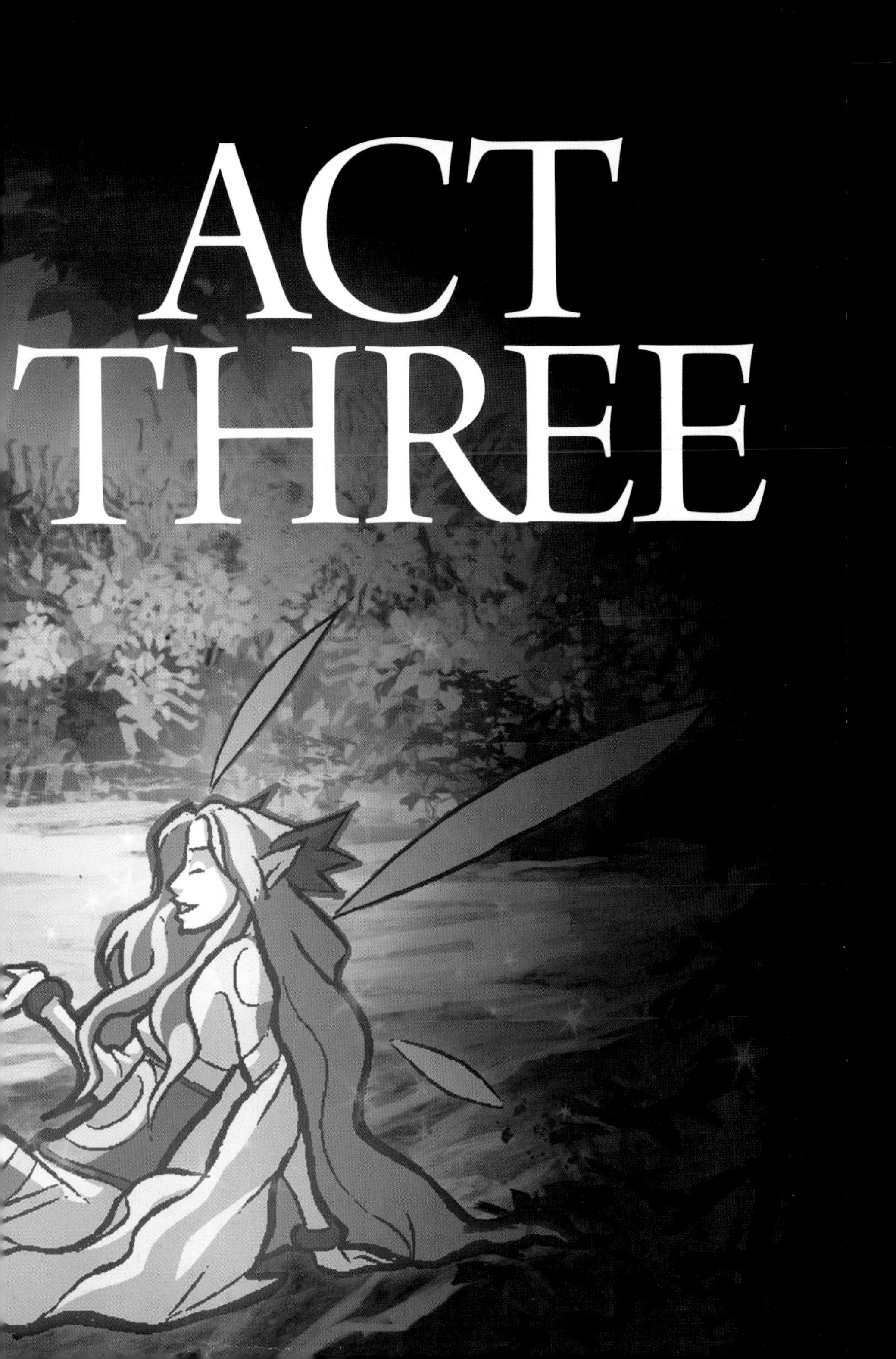

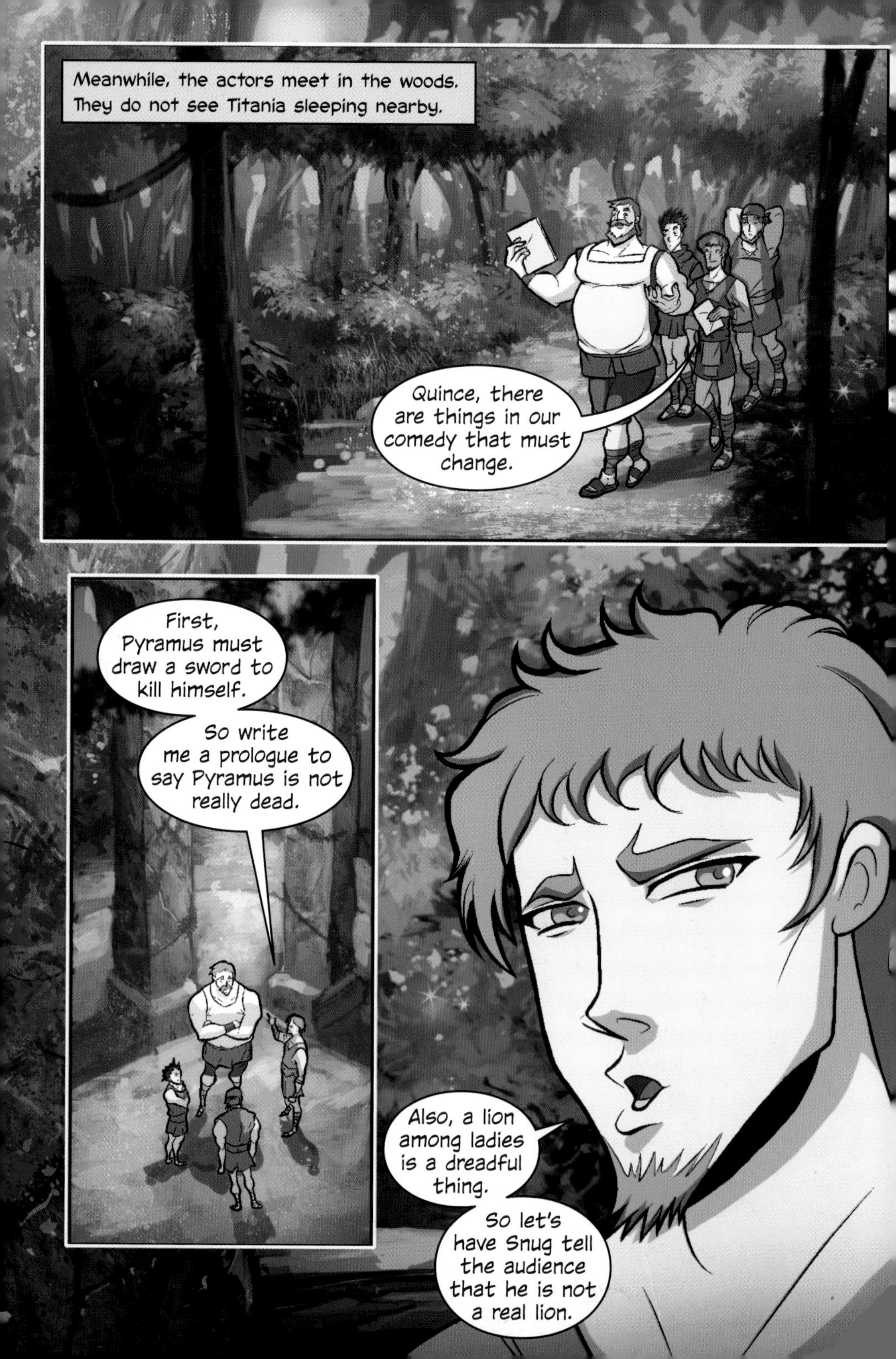
Meanwhile, the actors meet in the woods. They do not see Titania sleeping nearby.
Quince, there are things in our comedy that must change.
First, Pyramus must draw a sword to kill himself.
So write me a prologue to say Pyramus is not really dead.
Also, a lion among ladies is a dreadful thing.
So let's have Snug tell the audience that he is not a real lion.

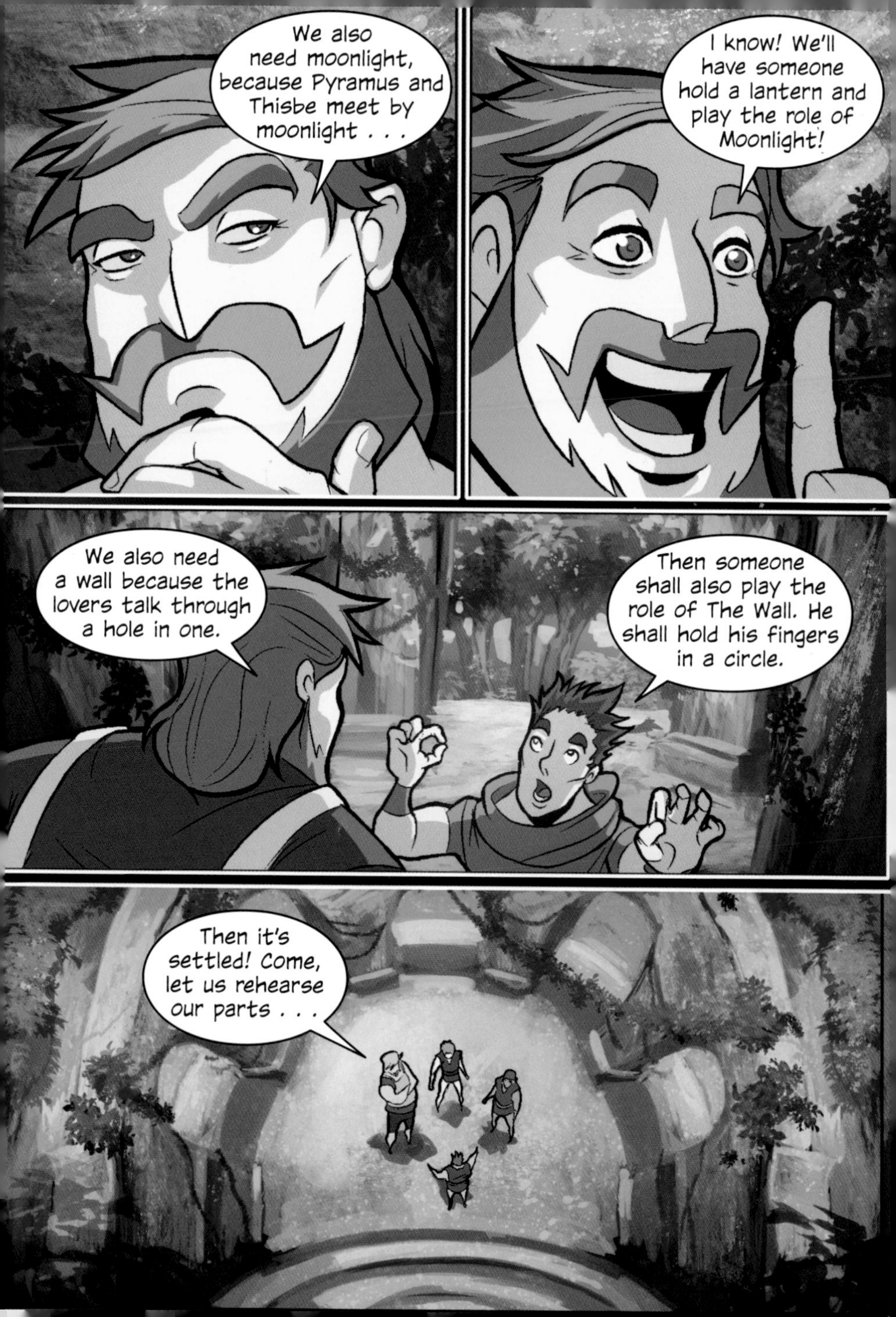
We also need moonlight, because Pyramus and Thisbe meet by moonlight . . .
I know! We'll have someone hold a lantern and play the role of Moonlight!
We also need a wall because the lovers talk through a hole in one.
Then someone shall also play the role of The Wall. He shall hold his fingers in a circle.
Then it's settled! Come, let us rehearse our parts . . .

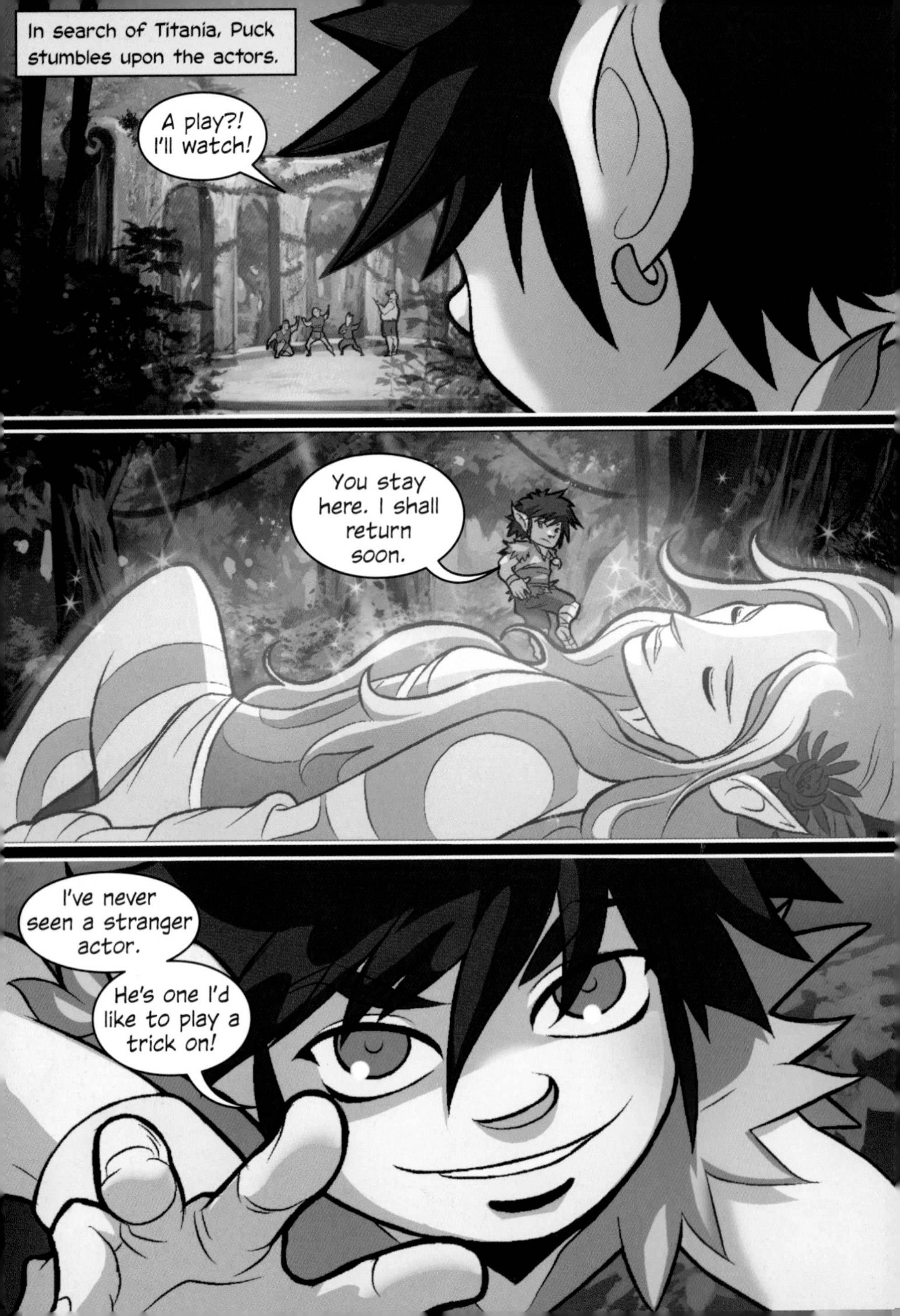
In search of Titania, Puck stumbles upon the actors.
A play?! I'll watch!
You stay here. I shall return soon.
I've never seen a stranger actor.
He's one I'd like to play a trick on!

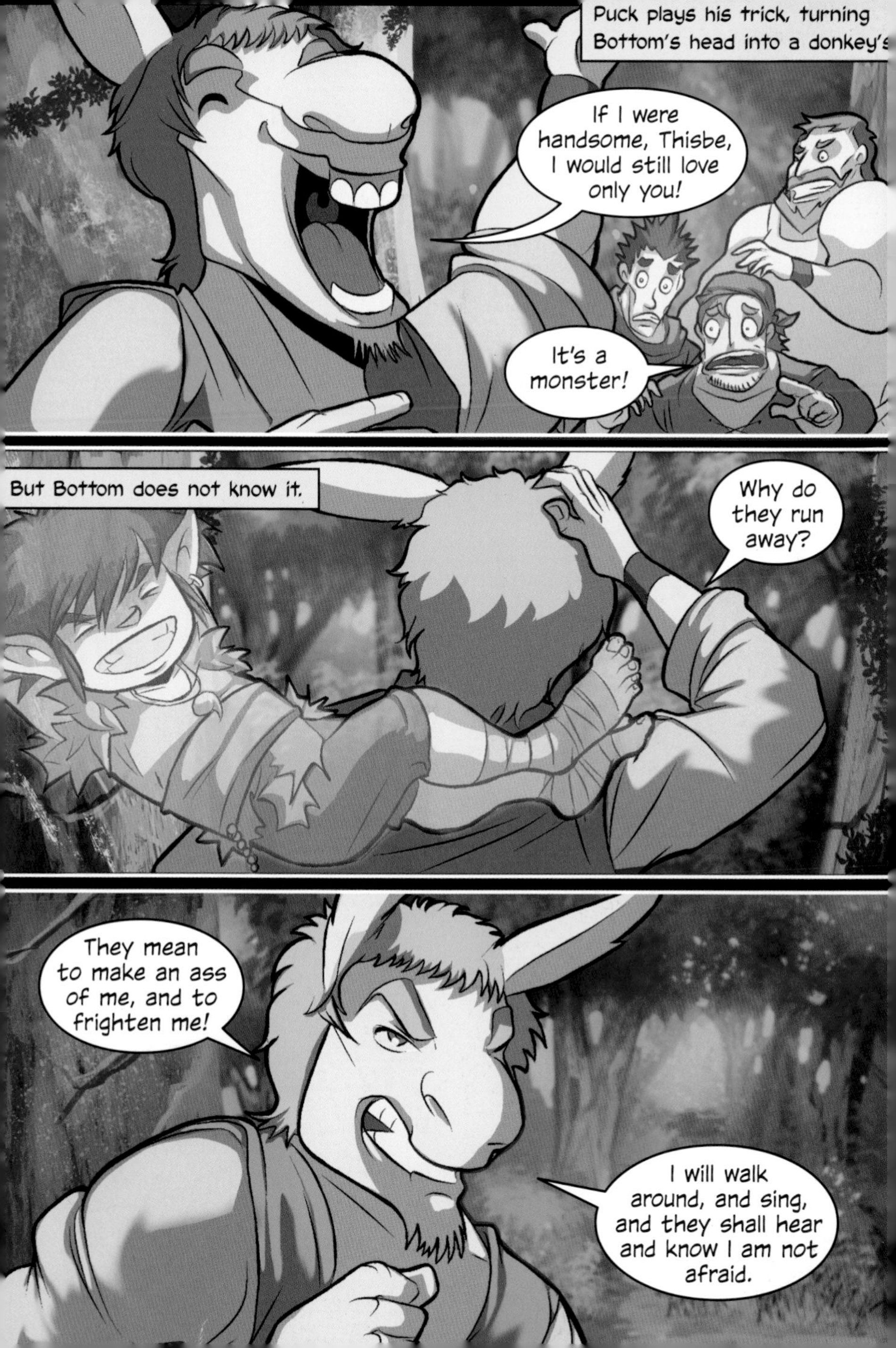

Puck plays his trick, turning Bottom's head into a donkey's
If I were handsome, Thisbe, I would still love only you!
It's a monster!
But Bottom does not know it.
Why do they run away?
They mean to make an ass of me, and to frighten me!
I will walk around, and sing, and they shall hear and know I am not afraid.

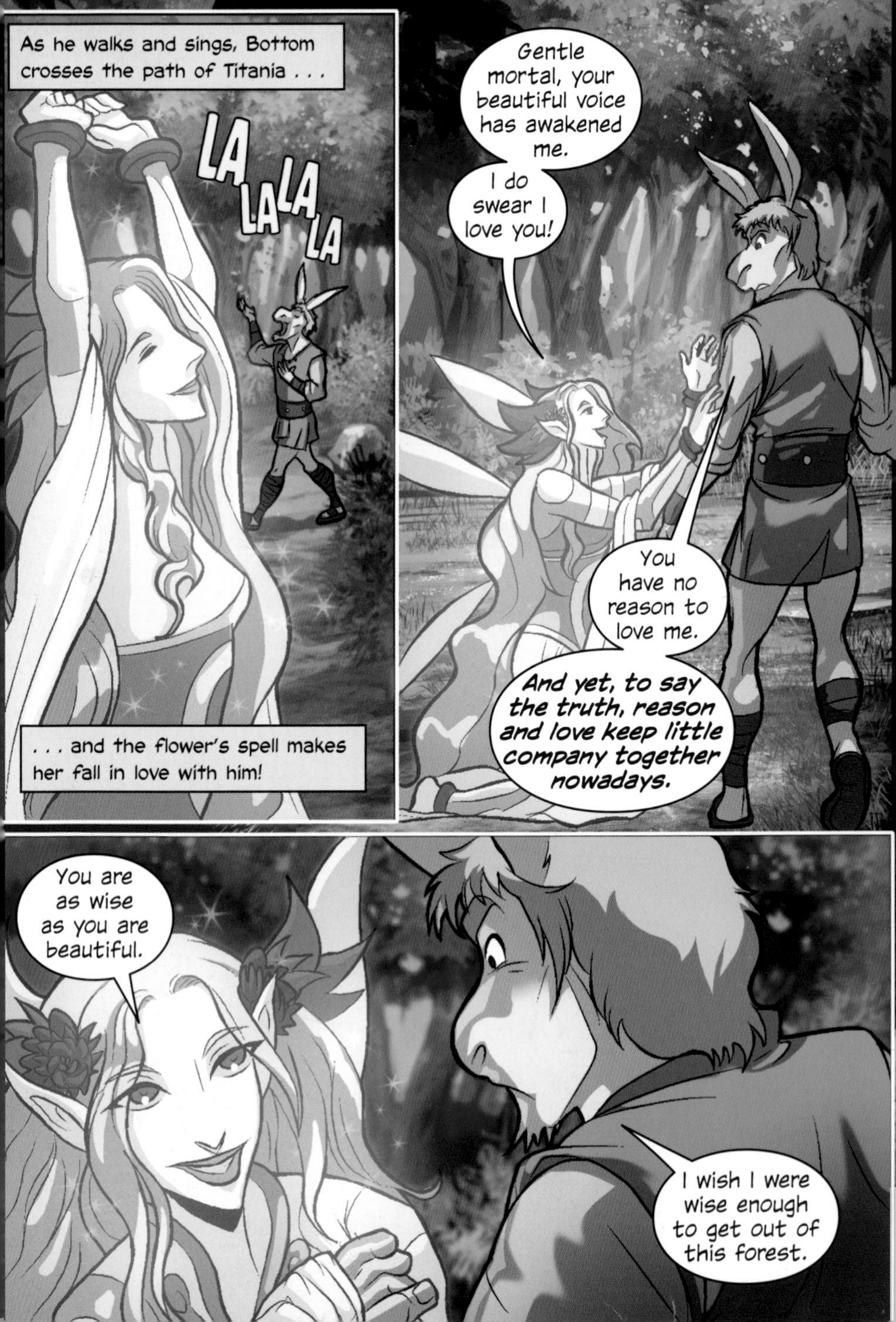
As he walks and sings, Bottom crosses the path of Titania . . .
LA LA LA LA LA
. . . and the flower's spell makes her fall in love with him!
Gentle mortal, your beautiful voice has awakened me.
I do swear I love you!
You have no reason to love me.
And yet, to say the truth, reason and love keep little company together nowadays.
You are as wise as you are beautiful.
I wish I were wise enough to get out of this forest.

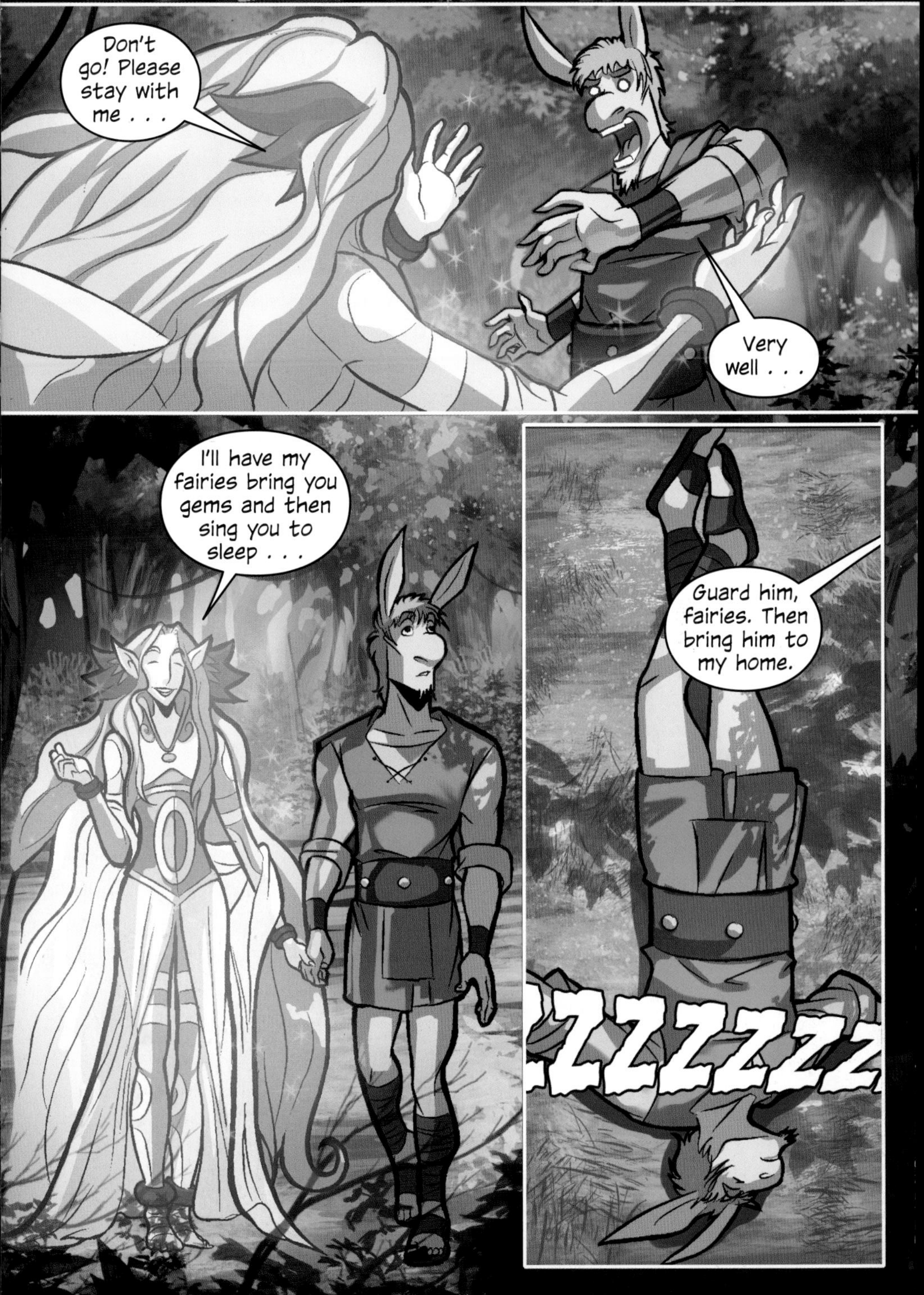
Don't go! Please stay with me . . .
Very well . . .
I'll have my fairies bring you gems and then sing you to sleep . . .
Guard him, fairies. Then bring him to my home.
ZZZZZZZ

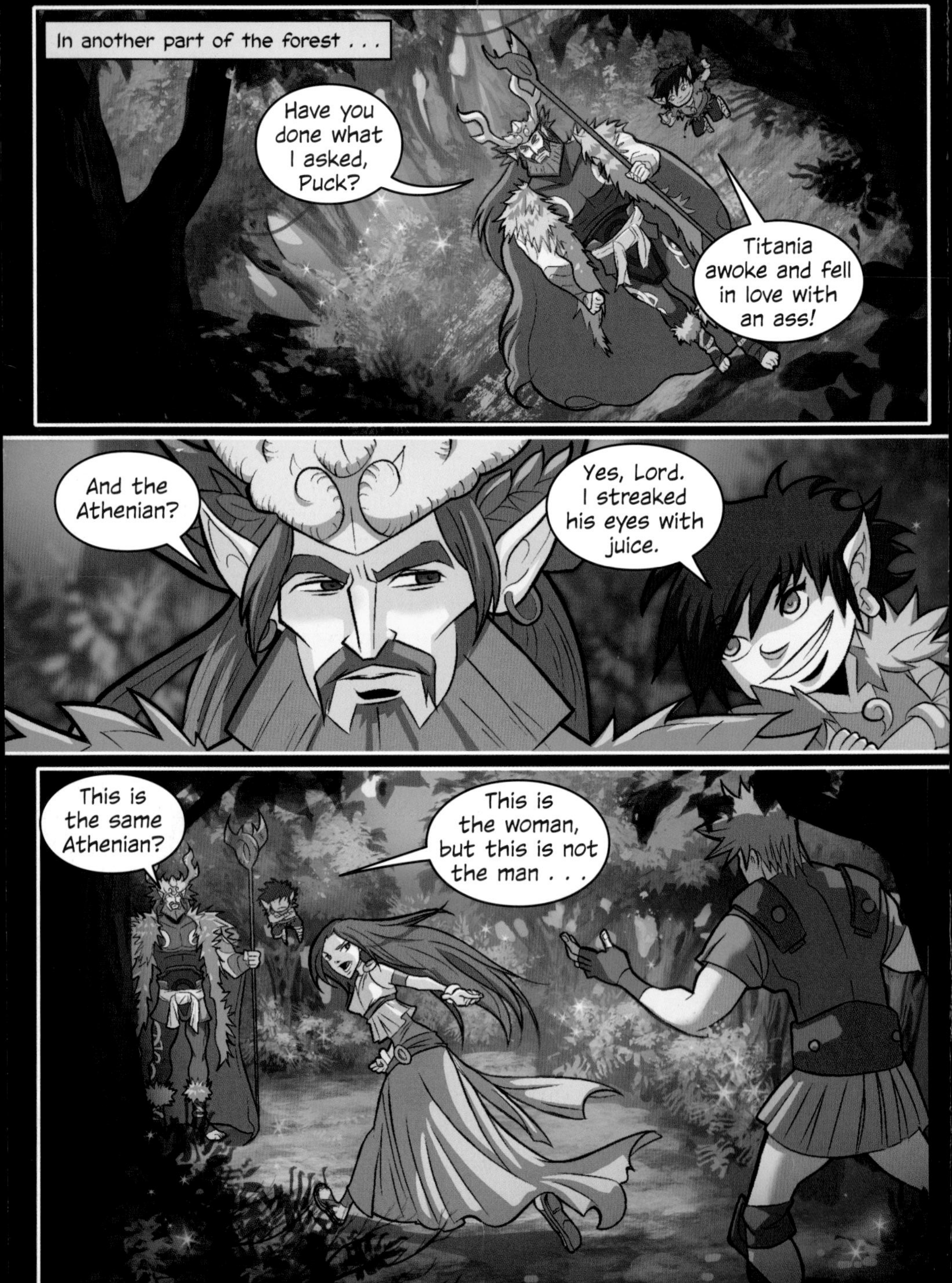
In another part of the forest . . .
Have you done what I asked, Puck?
Titania awoke and fell in love with an ass!
And the Athenian?
Yes, Lord. I streaked his eyes with juice.
This is the same Athenian?
This is the woman, but this is not the man . . .

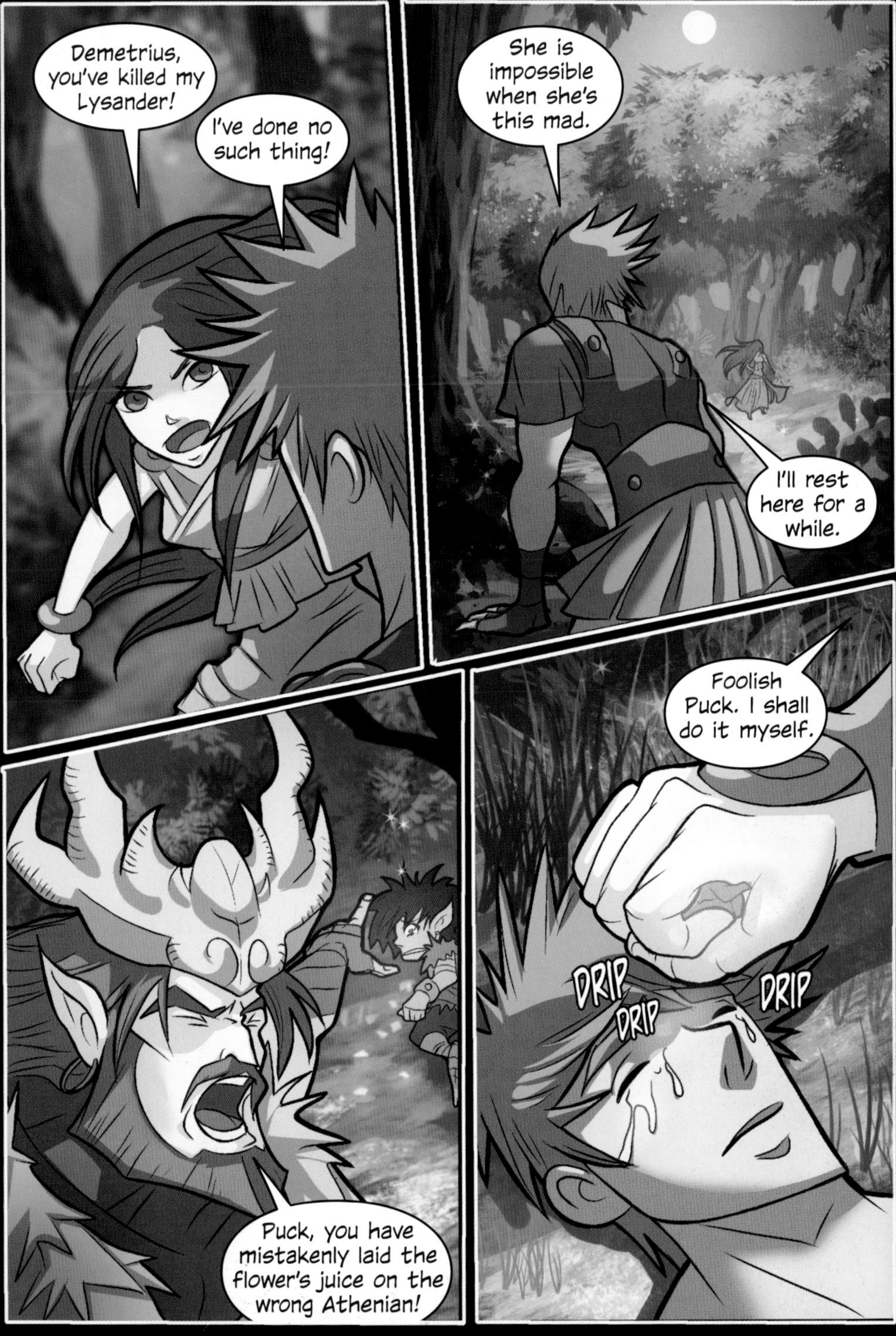
Demetrius, you've killed my Lysander!
I've done no such thing!
She is impossible when she's this mad.
I'll rest here for a while.
Puck, you have mistakenly laid the flower's juice on the wrong Athenian!
Foolish Puck. I shall do it myself.
DRIP
DRIP
DRIP

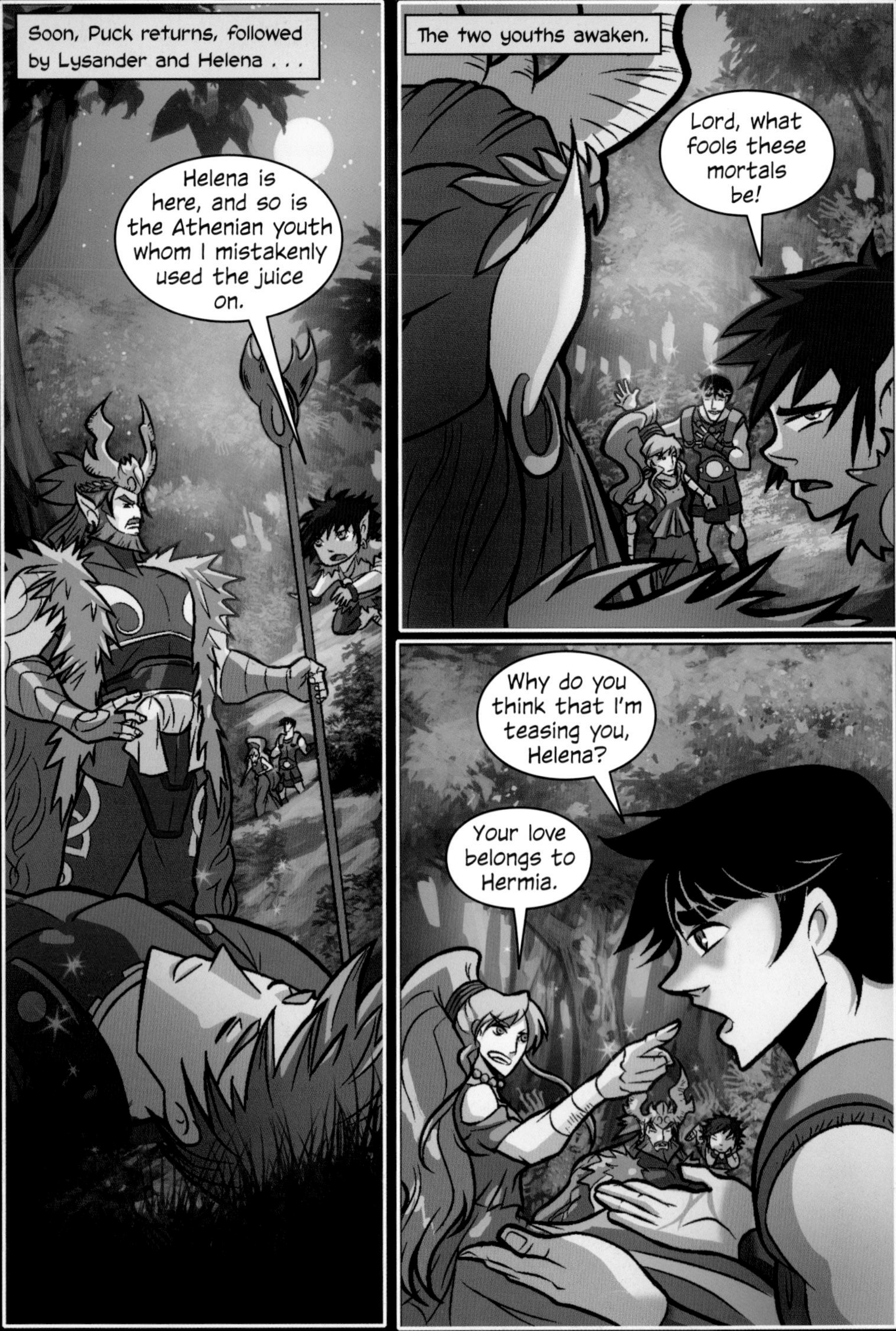
Soon, Puck returns, followed by Lysander and Helena . . .
Helena is here, and so is the Athenian youth whom I mistakenly used the juice on.
The two youths awaken.
Lord, what fools these mortals be!
Why do you think that I'm teasing you, Helena?
Your love belongs to Hermia.

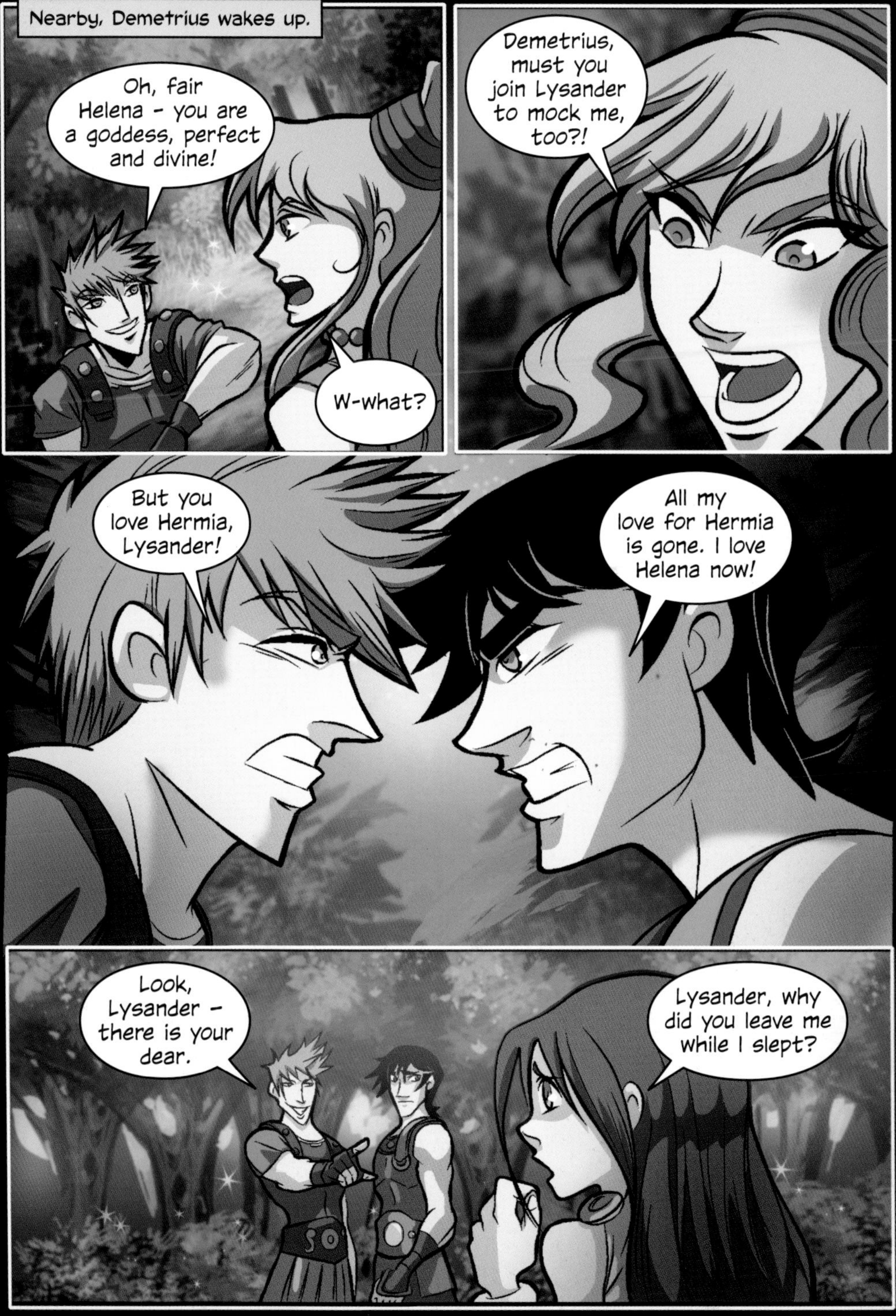
Nearby, Demetrius wakes up.
Oh, fair Helena - you are a goddess, perfect and divine!
W-what?
Demetrius, must you join Lysander to mock me, too?!
But you love Hermia, Lysander!
All my love for Hermia is gone. I love Helena now!
Look, Lysander - there is your dear.
Lysander, why did you leave me while I slept?

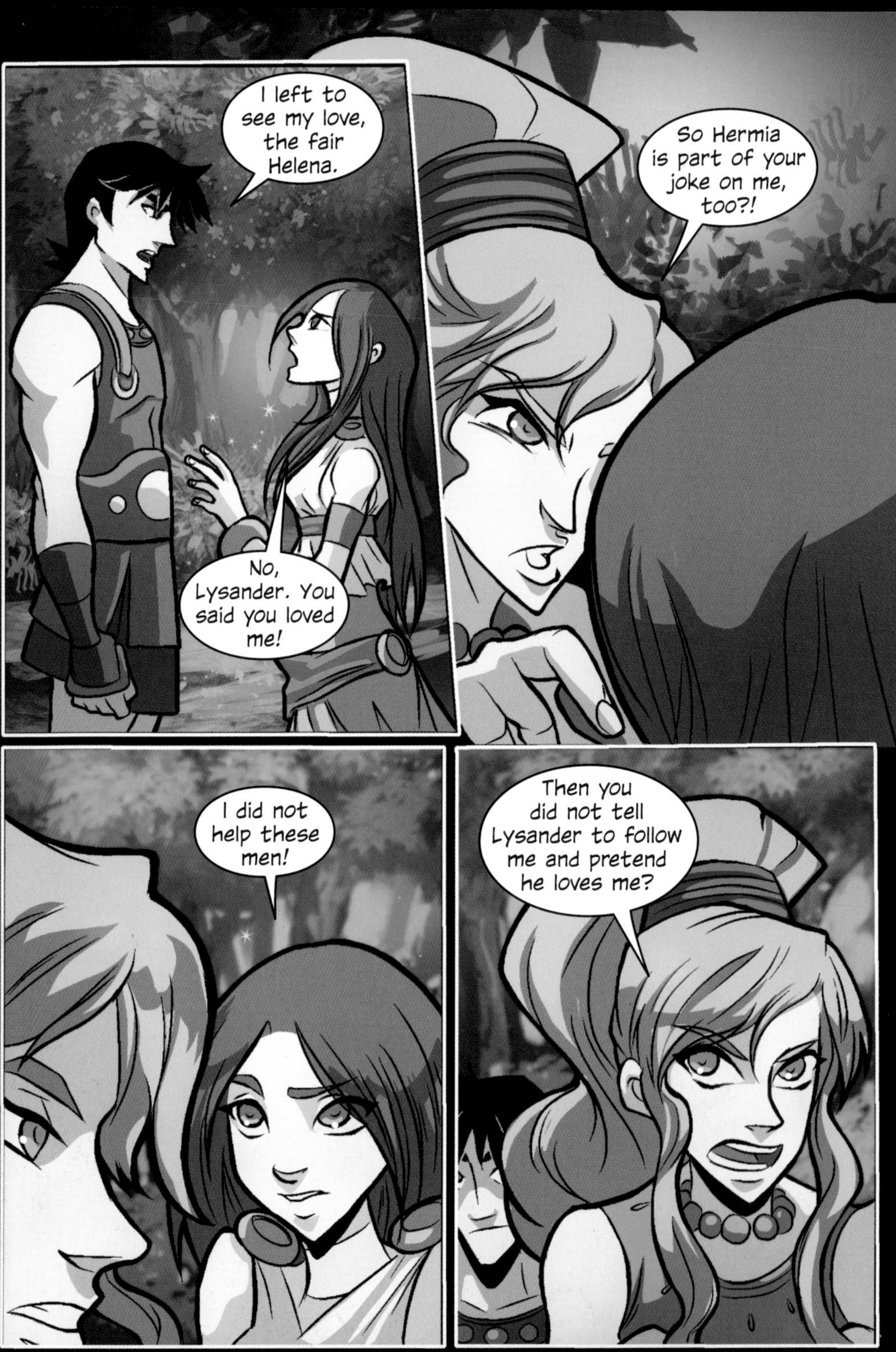
I left to see my love, the fair Helena.
No, Lysander. You said you loved me!
So Hermia is part of your joke on me, too?!
I did not help these men!
Then you did not tell Lysander to follow me and pretend he loves me?

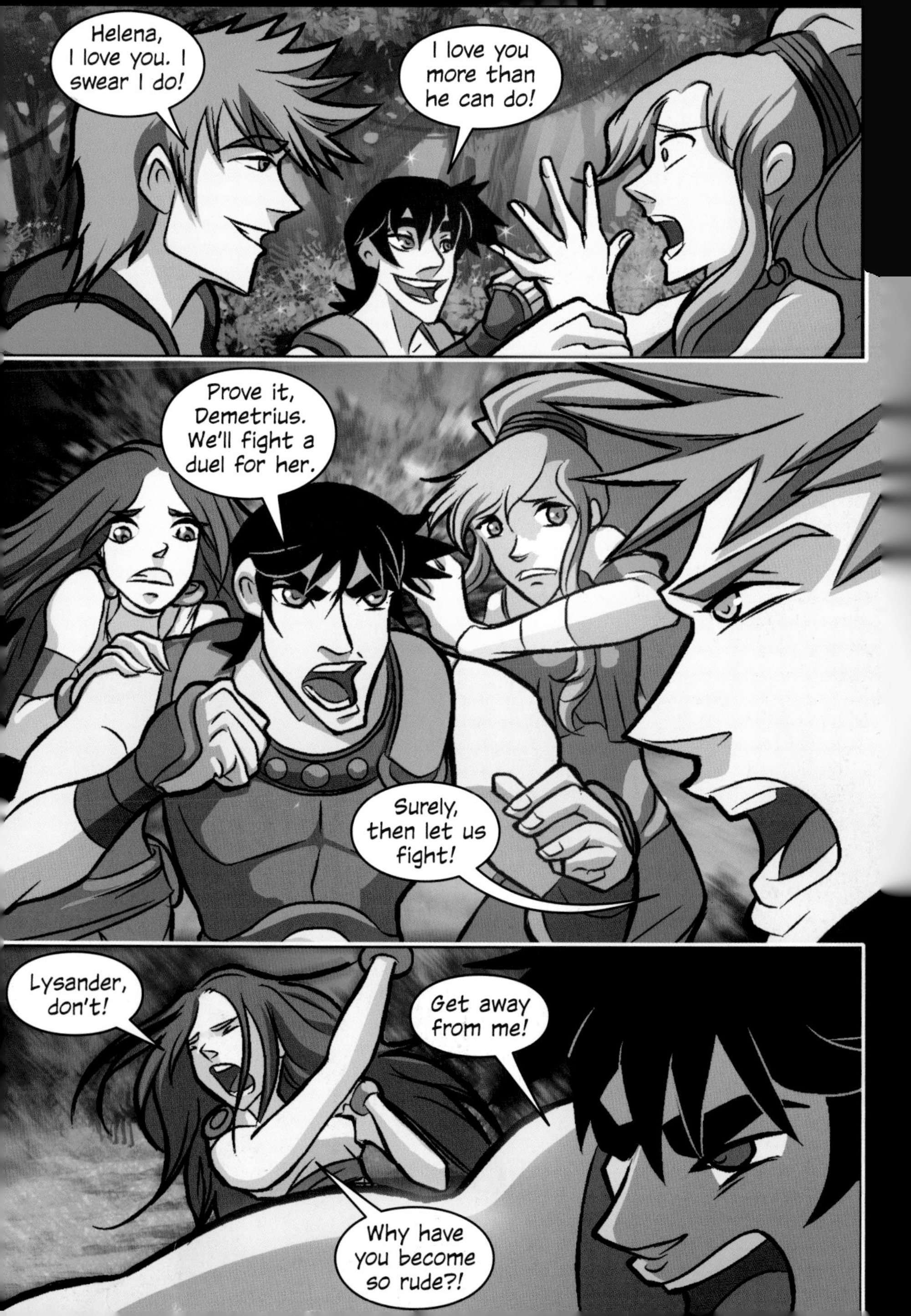
Helena, I love you. I swear I do!
I love you more than he can do!
Prove it, Demetrius. We'll fight a duel for her.
Surely, then let us fight!
Lysander, don't!
Get away from me!
Why have you become so rude?!

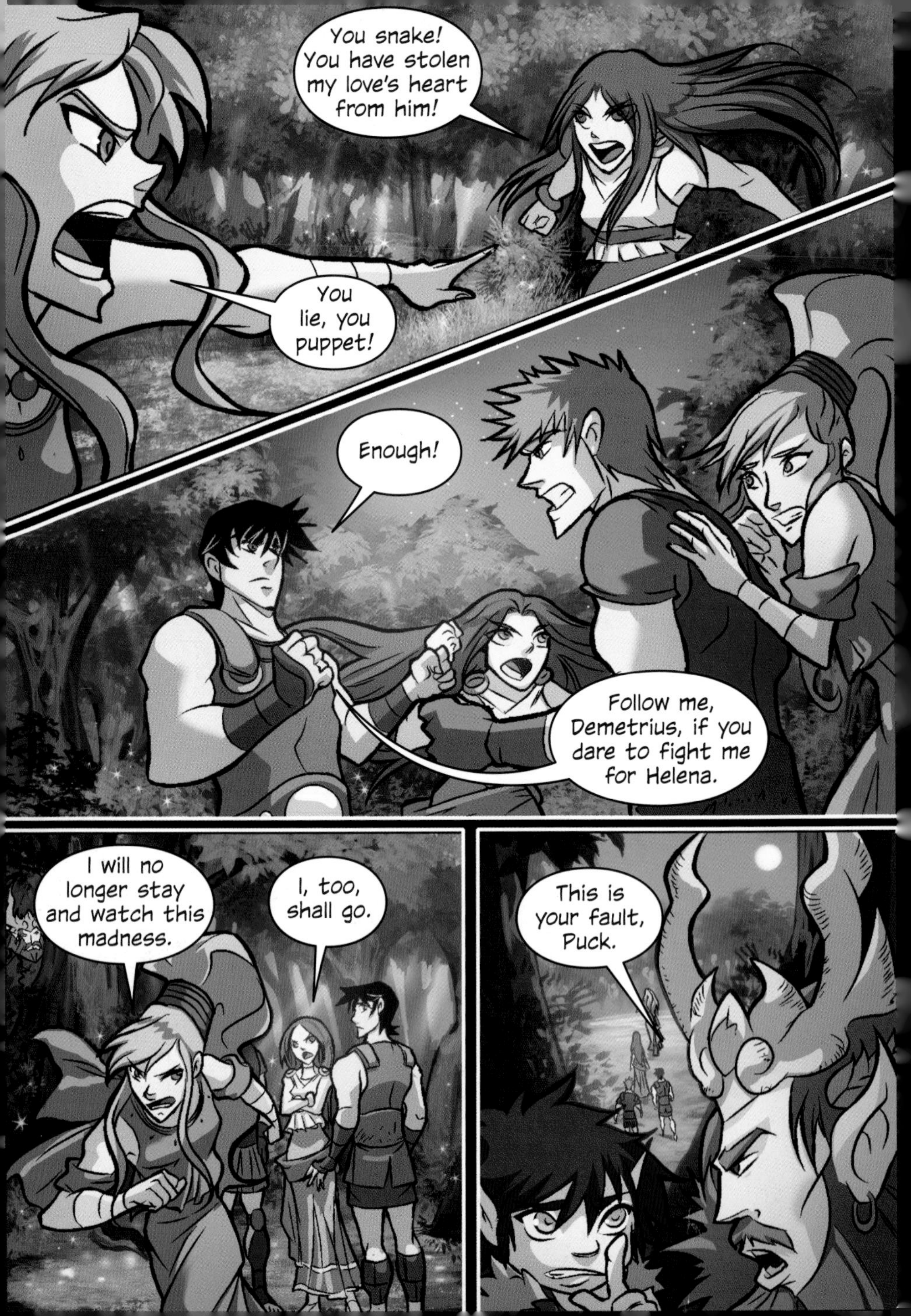
You snake! You have stolen my love's heart from him!
You lie, you puppet!
Enough!
Follow me, Demetrius, if you dare to fight me for Helena.
I will no longer stay and watch this madness.
I, too, shall go.
This is your fault, Puck.

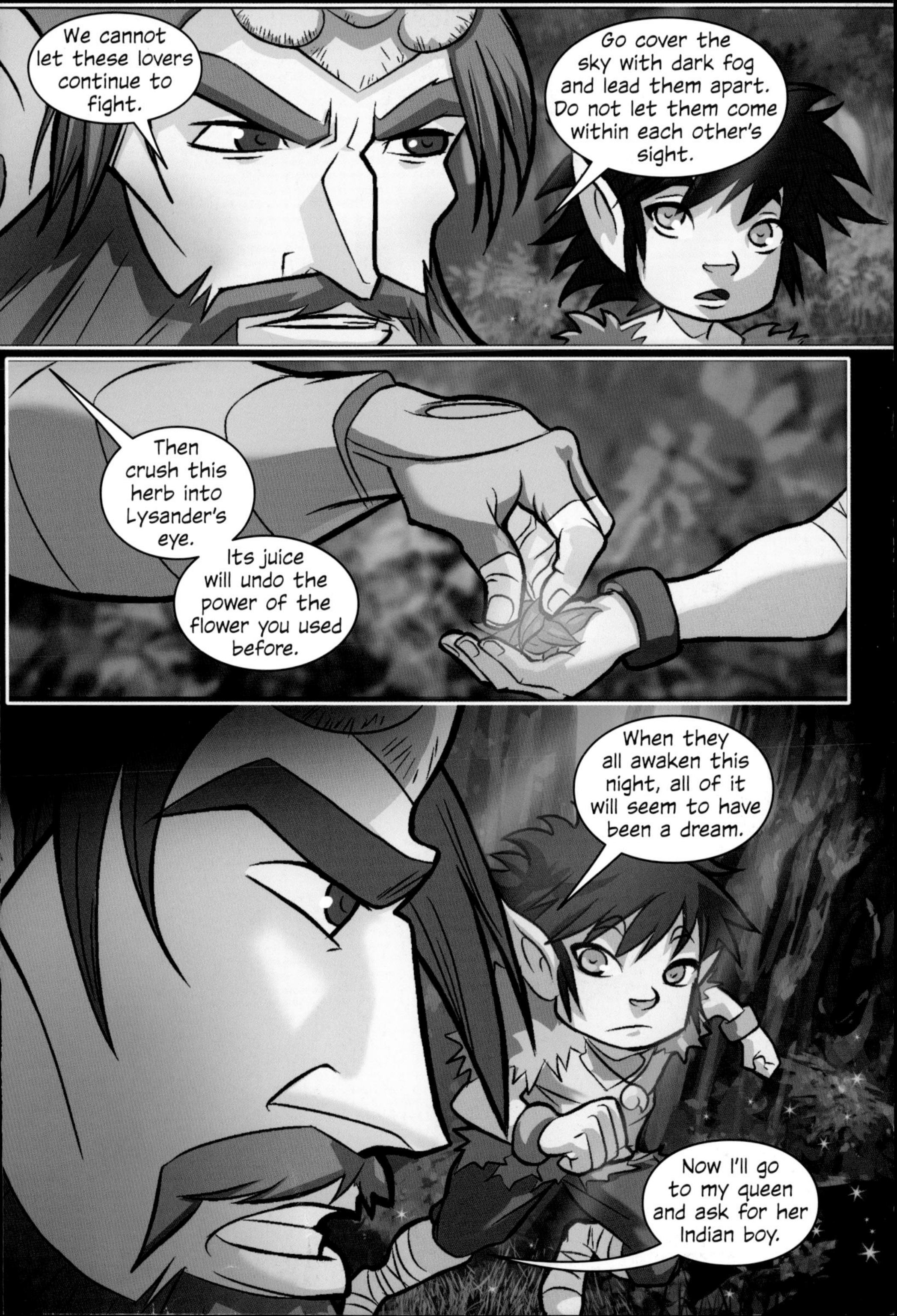
We cannot let these lovers continue to fight.
Go cover the sky with dark fog and lead them apart. Do not let them come within each other's sight.
Then crush this herb into Lysander's eye.
Its juice will undo the power of the flower you used before.
When they all awaken this night, all of it will seem to have been a dream.
Now I'll go to my queen and ask for her Indian boy.

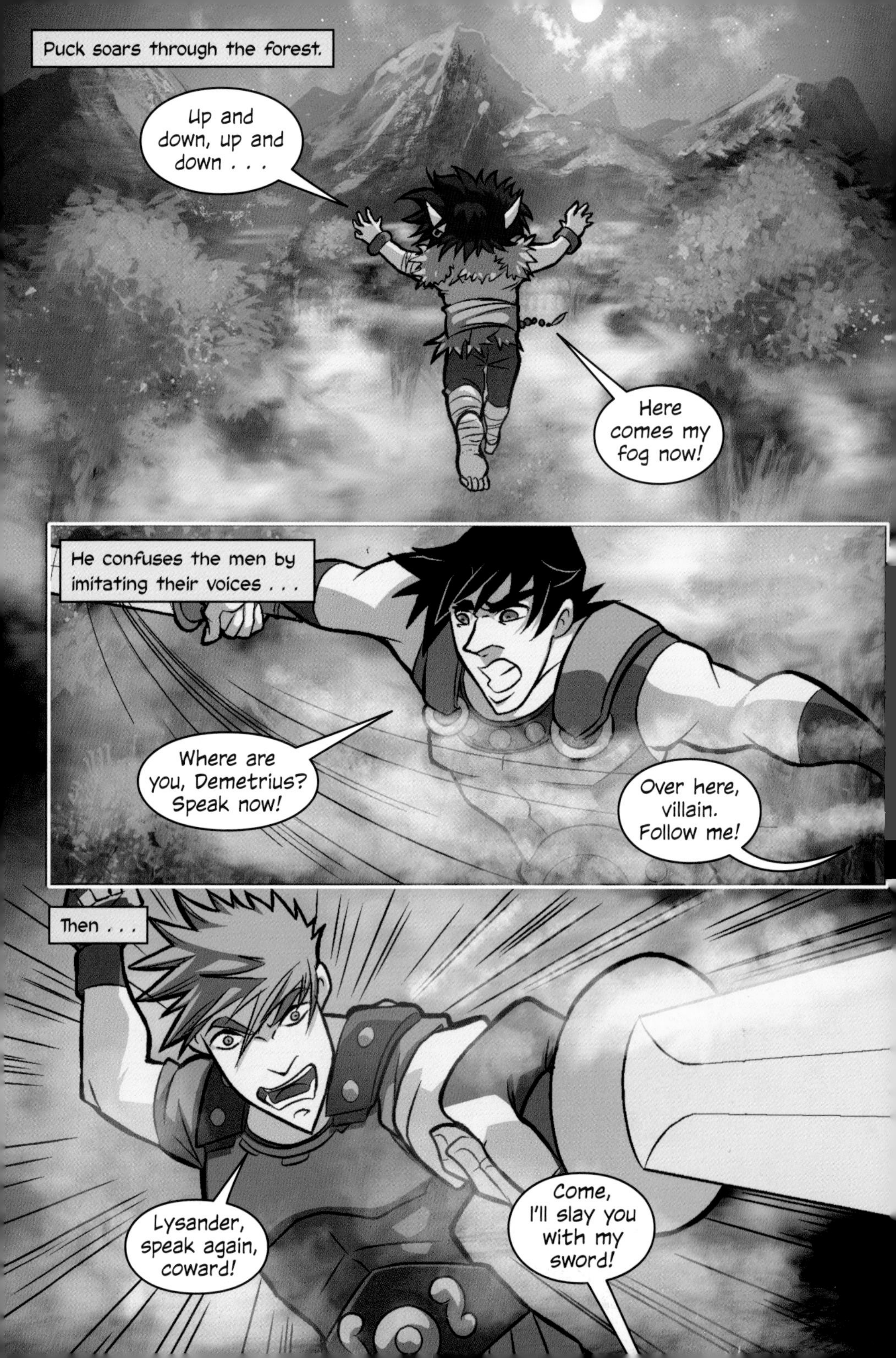
Puck soars through the forest.
Up and down, up and down . . .
Here comes my fog now!
He confuses the men by imitating their voices . . .
Where are you, Demetrius? Speak now!
Over here, villain. Follow me!
Then . . .
Lysander, speak again, coward!
Come, I'll slay you with my sword!

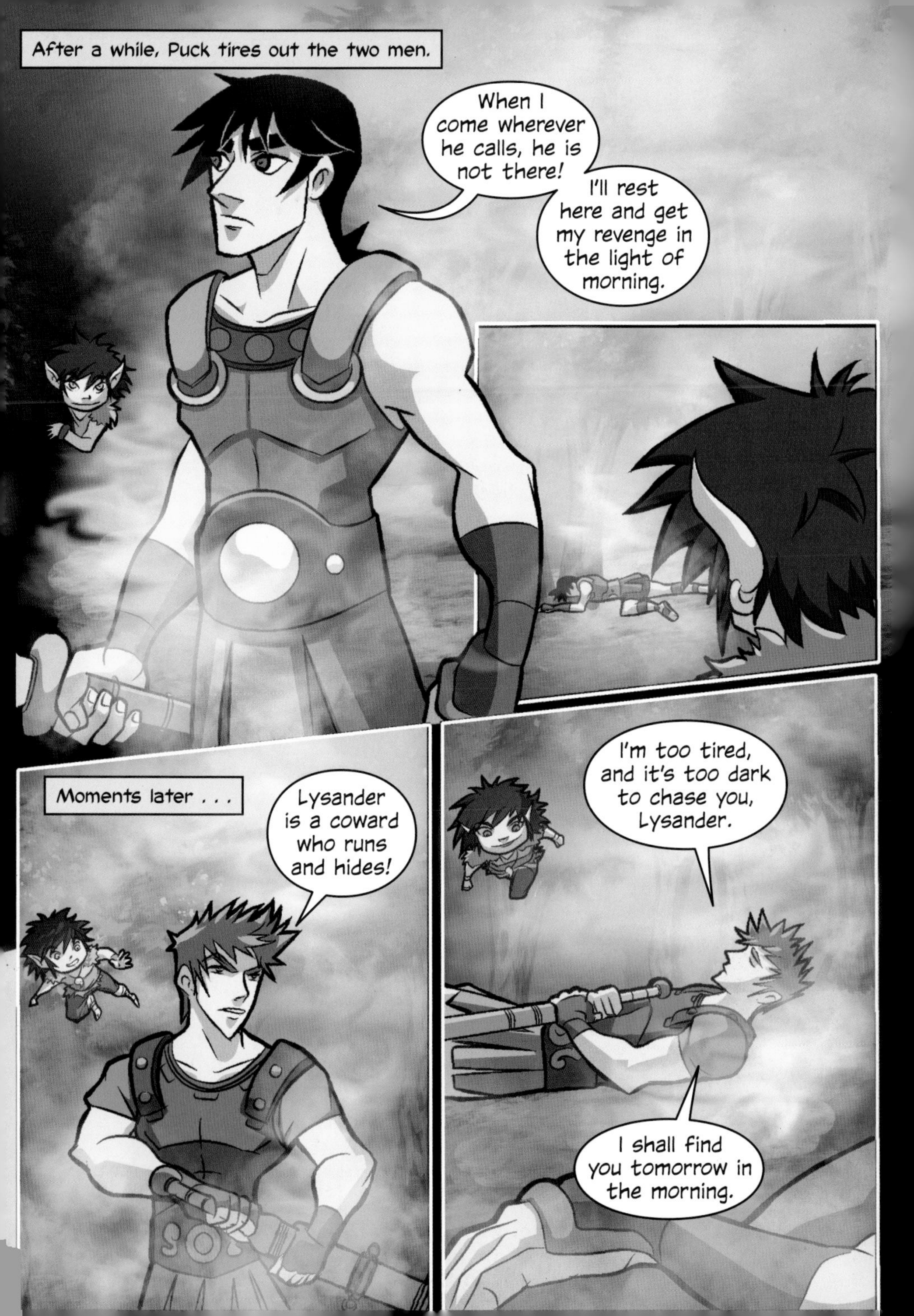
After a while, Puck tires out the two men.
When I come wherever he calls, he is not there!
I'll rest here and get my revenge in the light of morning.
Moments later . . .
Lysander is a coward who runs and hides!
I'm too tired, and it's too dark to chase you, Lysander.
I shall find you tomorrow in the morning.

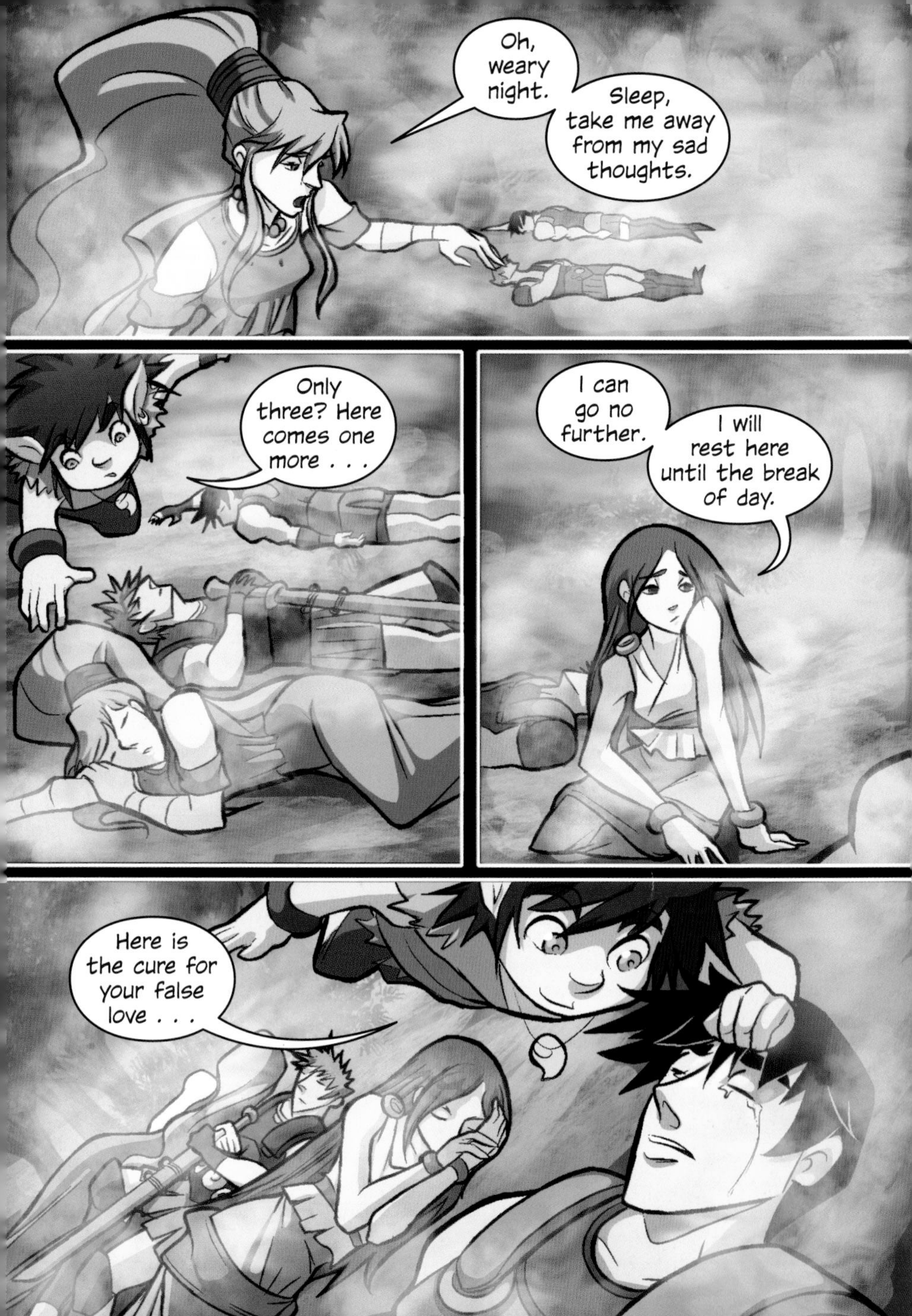
Oh, weary night.
Sleep, take me away from my sad thoughts.
Only three? Here comes one more . . .
I can go no further.
I will rest here until the break of day.
Here is the cure for your false love . . .

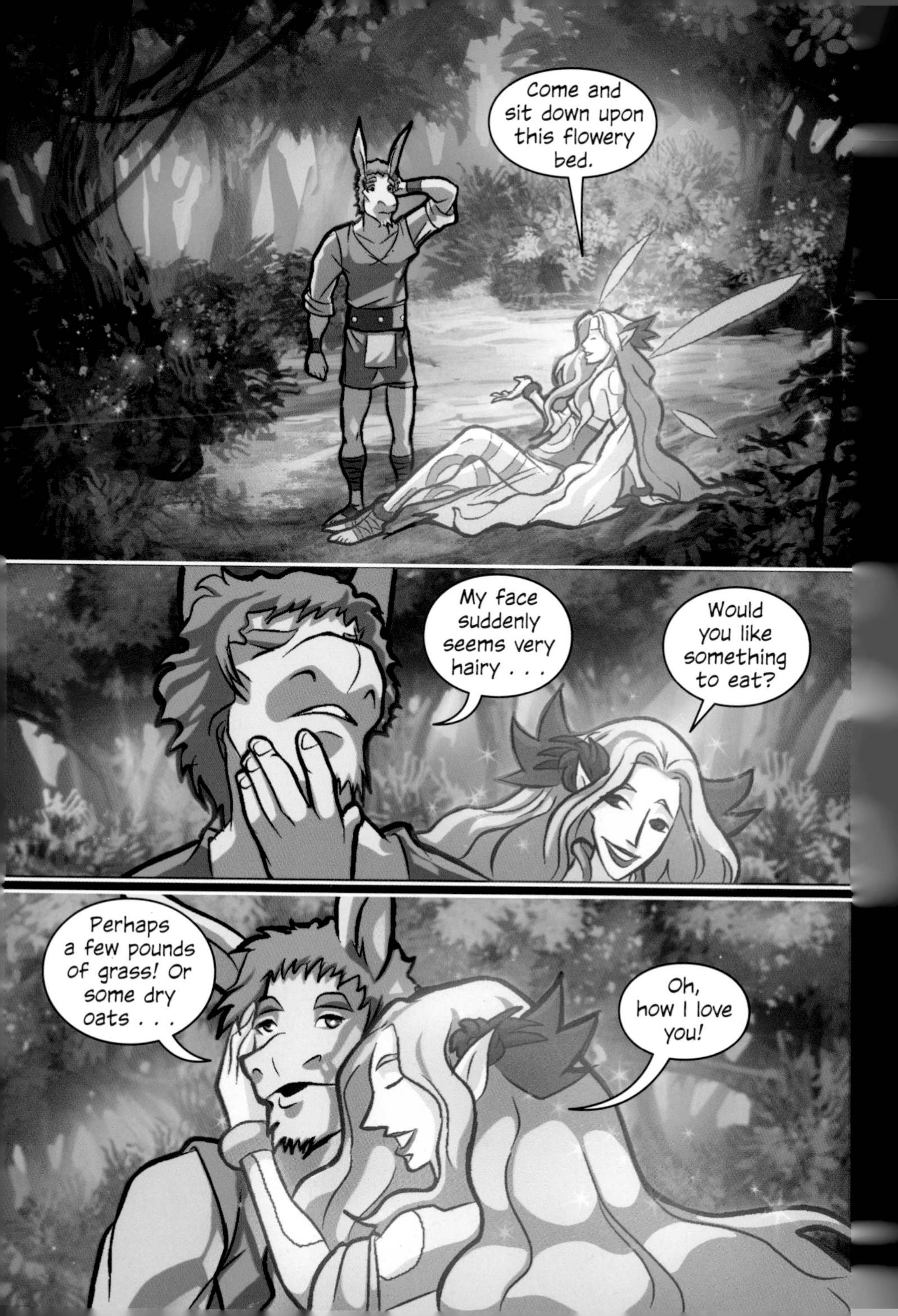
Come and sit down upon this flowery bed.
My face suddenly seems very hairy . . .
Would you like something to eat?
Perhaps a few pounds of grass! Or some dry oats . . .
Oh, how I love you!

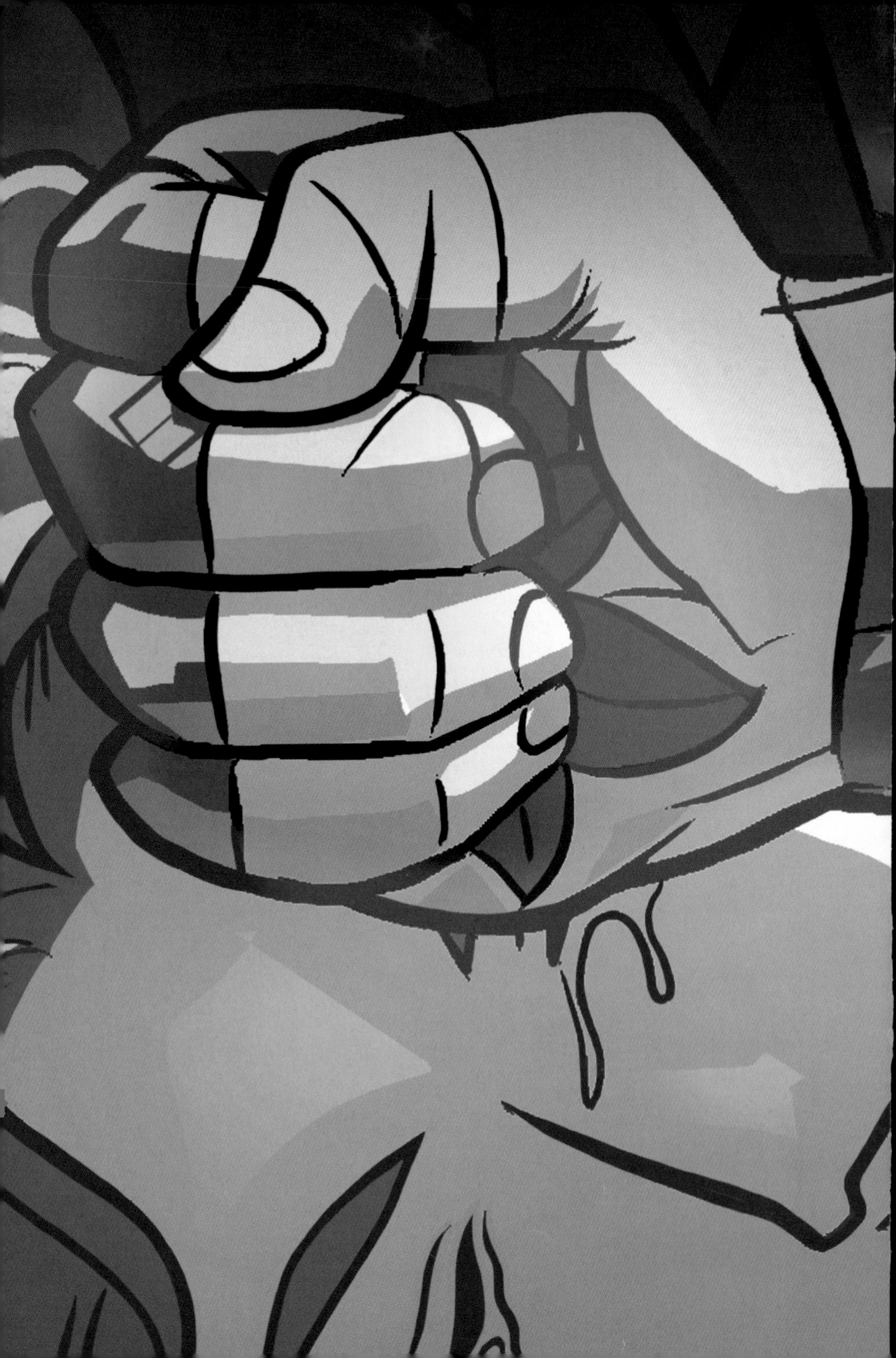

ACT FOUR

"I have had a dream, past the wit of man to say what dream it was."

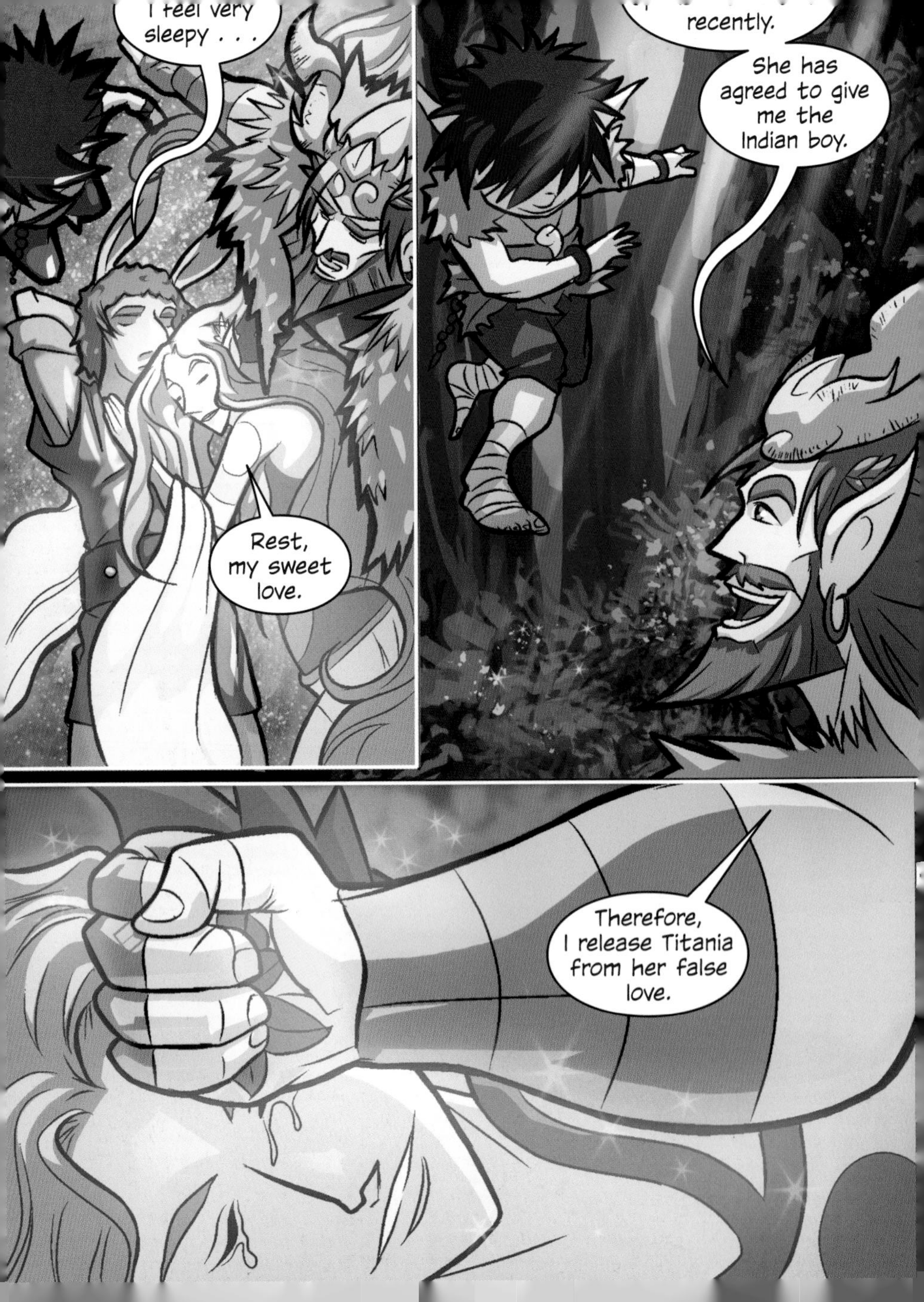

I feel very sleepy . . .
Rest, my sweet love.
recently.
She has agreed to give me the Indian boy.
Therefore, I release Titania from her false love.

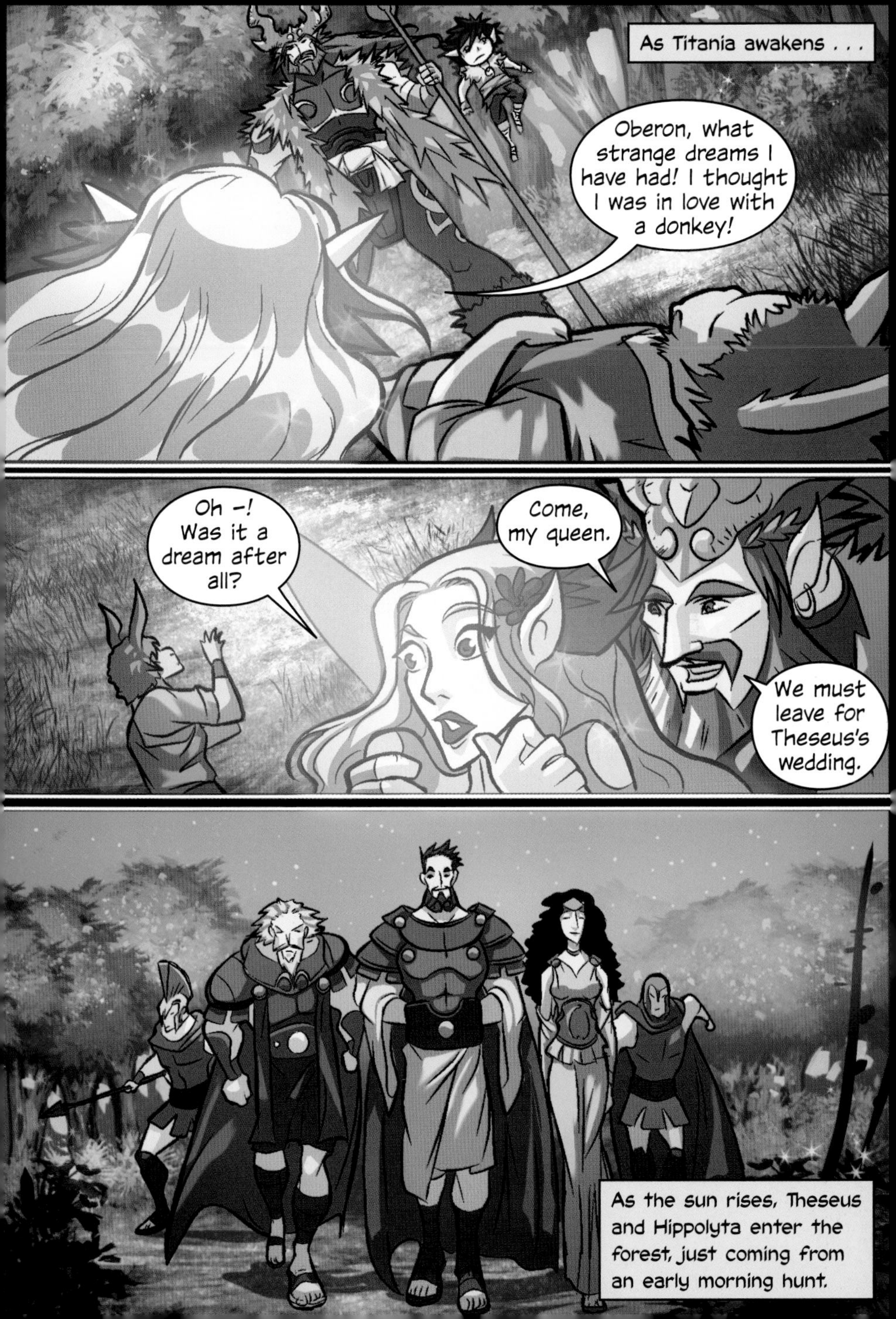
As Titania awakens . . .
Oberon, what strange dreams I have had! I thought I was in love with a donkey!
Oh –! Was it a dream after all?
Come, my queen.
We must leave for Theseus's wedding.
As the sun rises, Theseus and Hippolyta enter the forest, just coming from an early morning hunt.

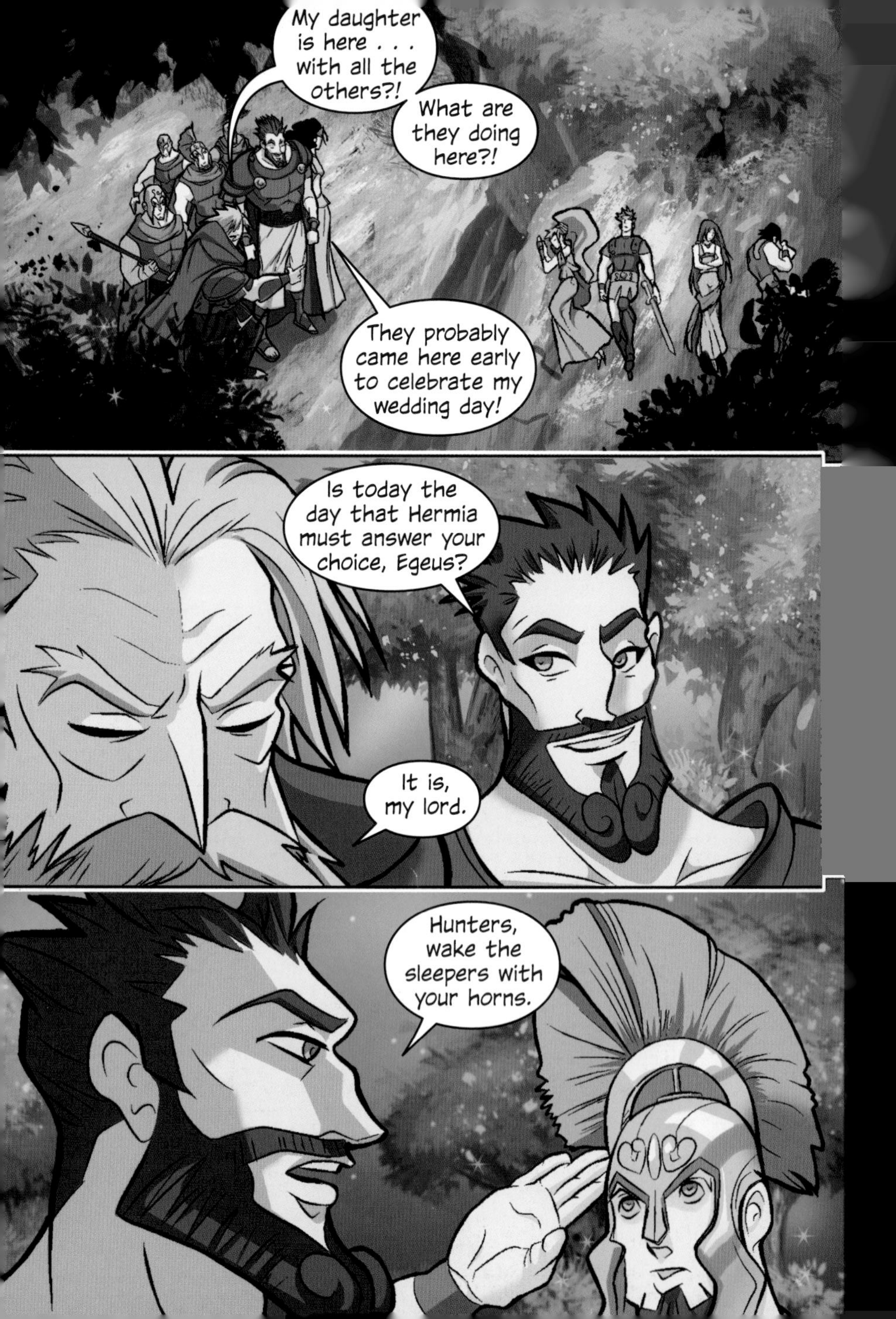
My daughter is here . . . with all the others?!
What are they doing here?!
They probably came here early to celebrate my wedding day!
Is today the day that Hermia must answer your choice, Egeus?
It is, my lord.
Hunters, wake the sleepers with your horns.

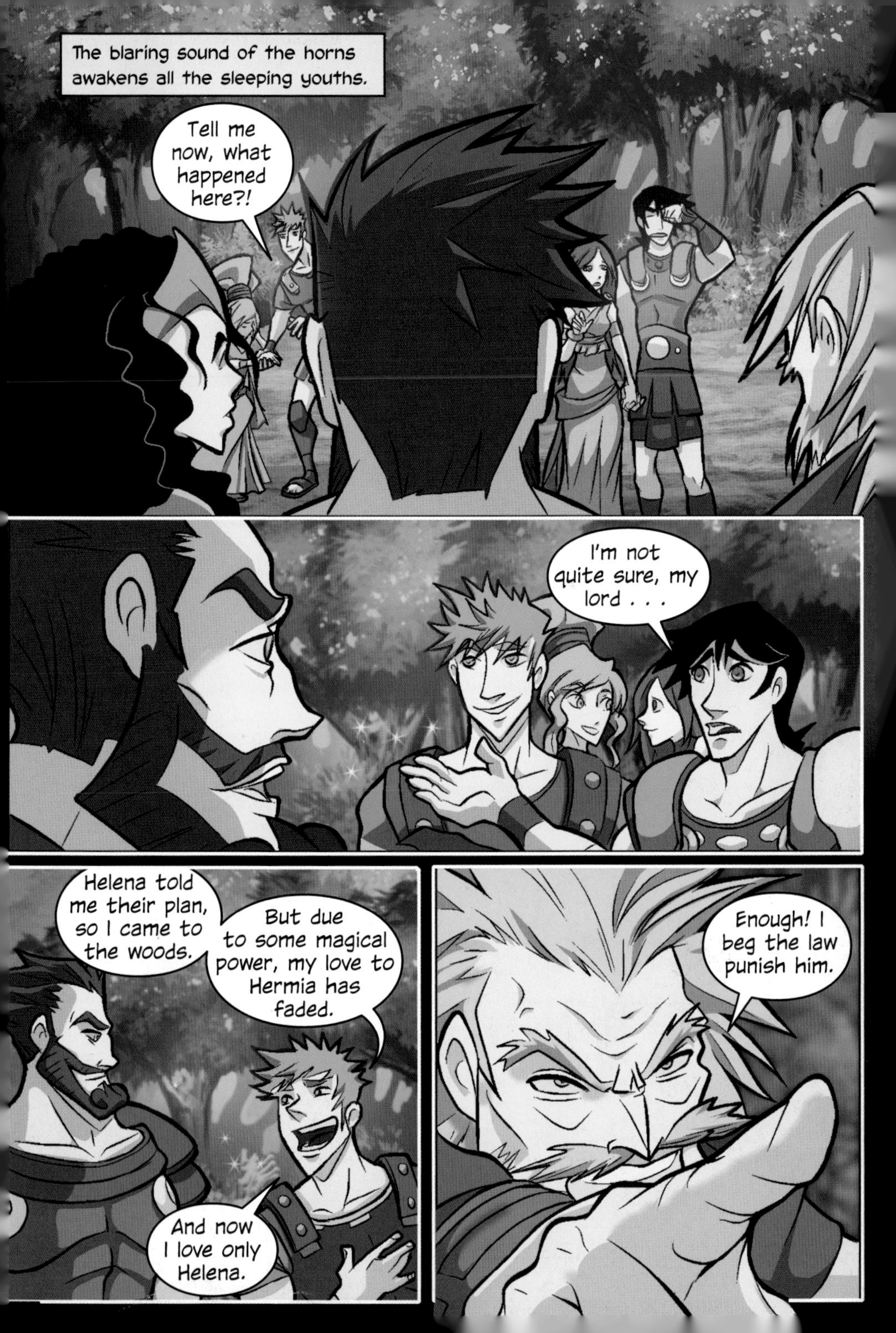
The blaring sound of the horns awakens all the sleeping youths.
Tell me now, what happened here?!
I'm not quite sure, my lord . . .
Helena told me their plan, so I came to the woods.
But due to some magical power, my love to Hermia has faded.
And now I love only Helena.
Enough! I beg the law punish him.

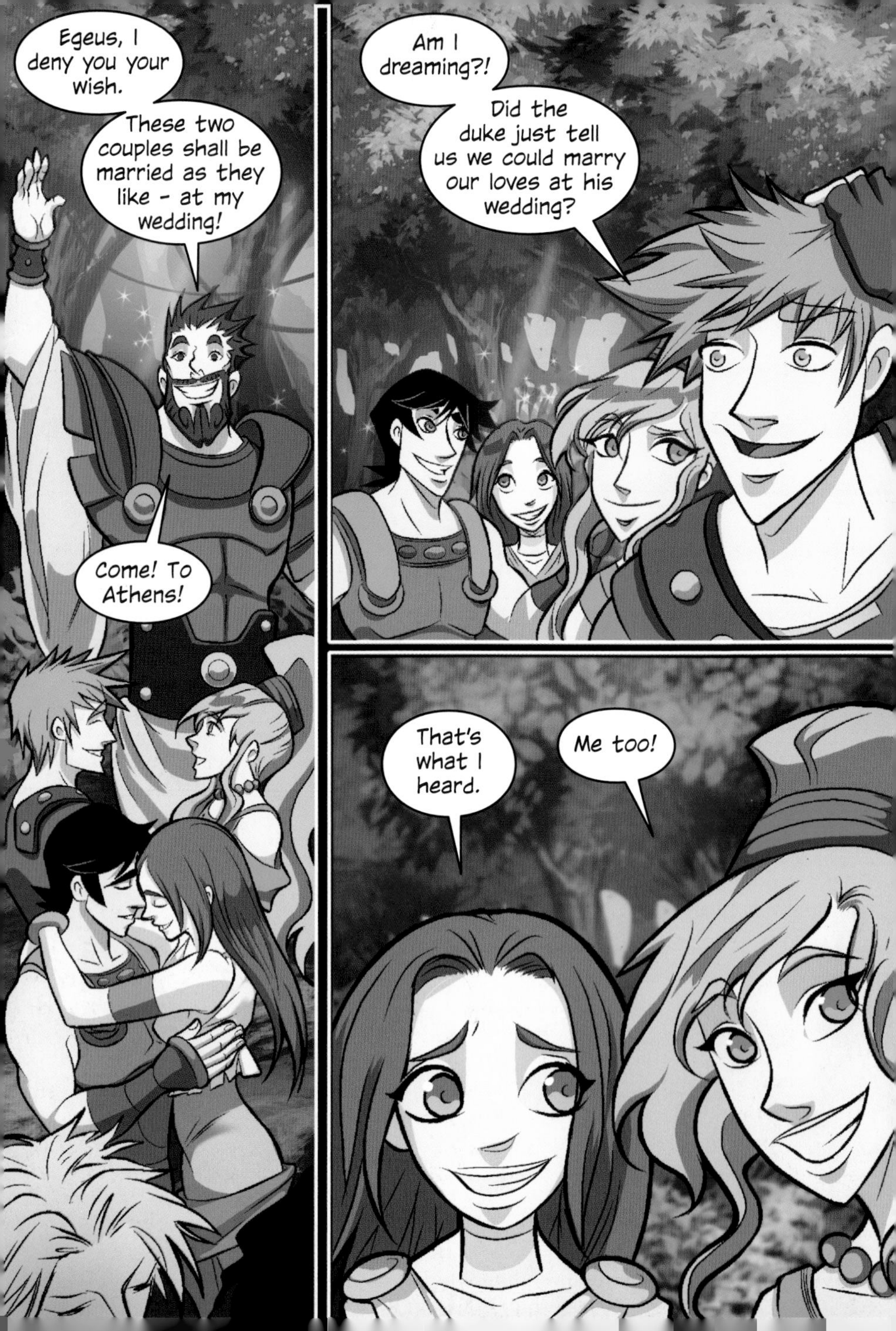
Egeus, I deny you your wish.
These two couples shall be married as they like - at my wedding!
Come! To Athens!
Am I dreaming?!
Did the duke just tell us we could marry our loves at his wedding?
That's what I heard.
Me too!

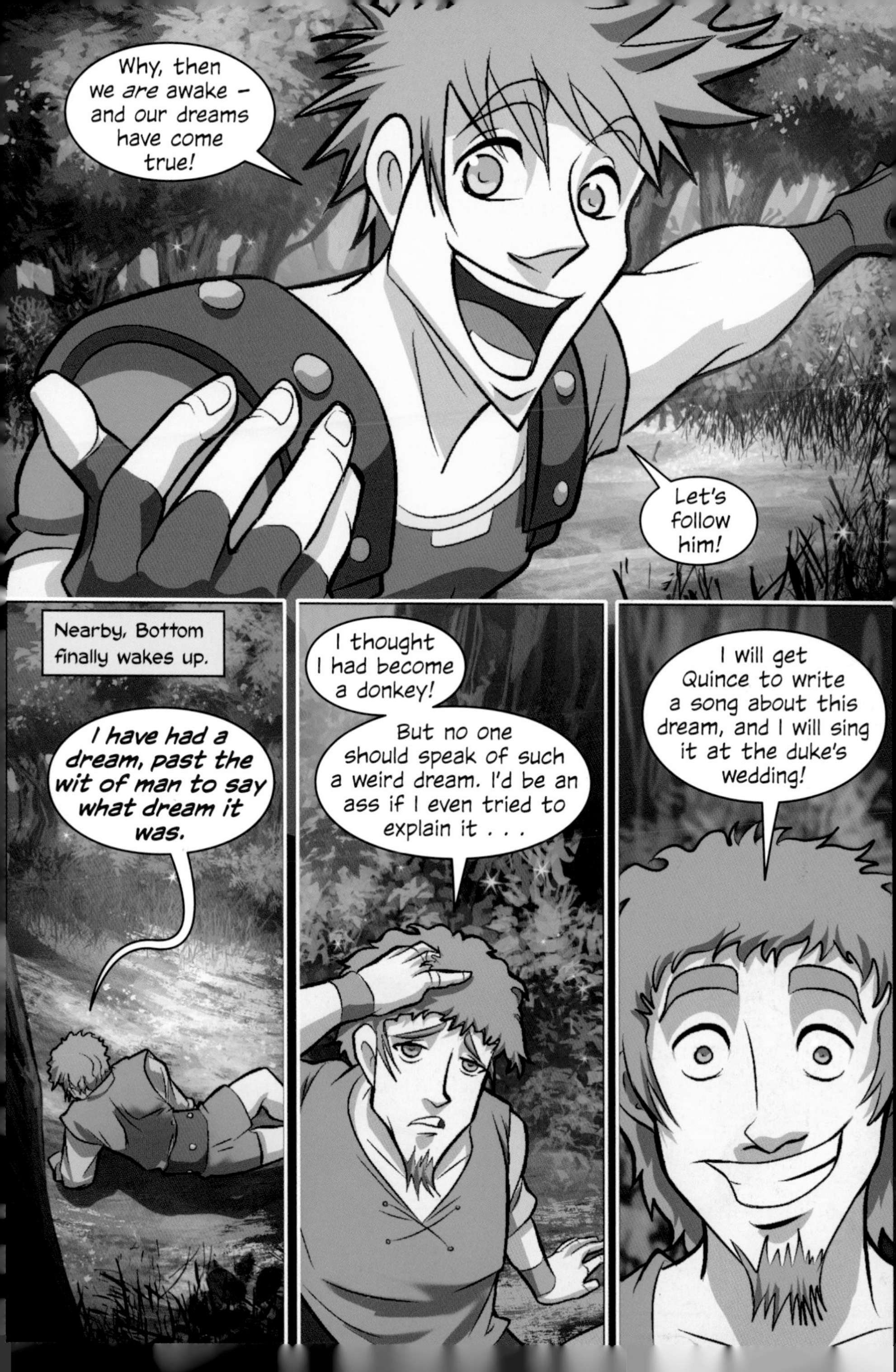

Why, then we *are* awake – and our dreams have come true!
Let's follow him!
Nearby, Bottom finally wakes up.
I have had a dream, past the wit of man to say what dream it was.
I thought I had become a donkey!
But no one should speak of such a weird dream. I'd be an ass if I even tried to explain it . . .
I will get Quince to write a song about this dream, and I will sing it at the duke's wedding!

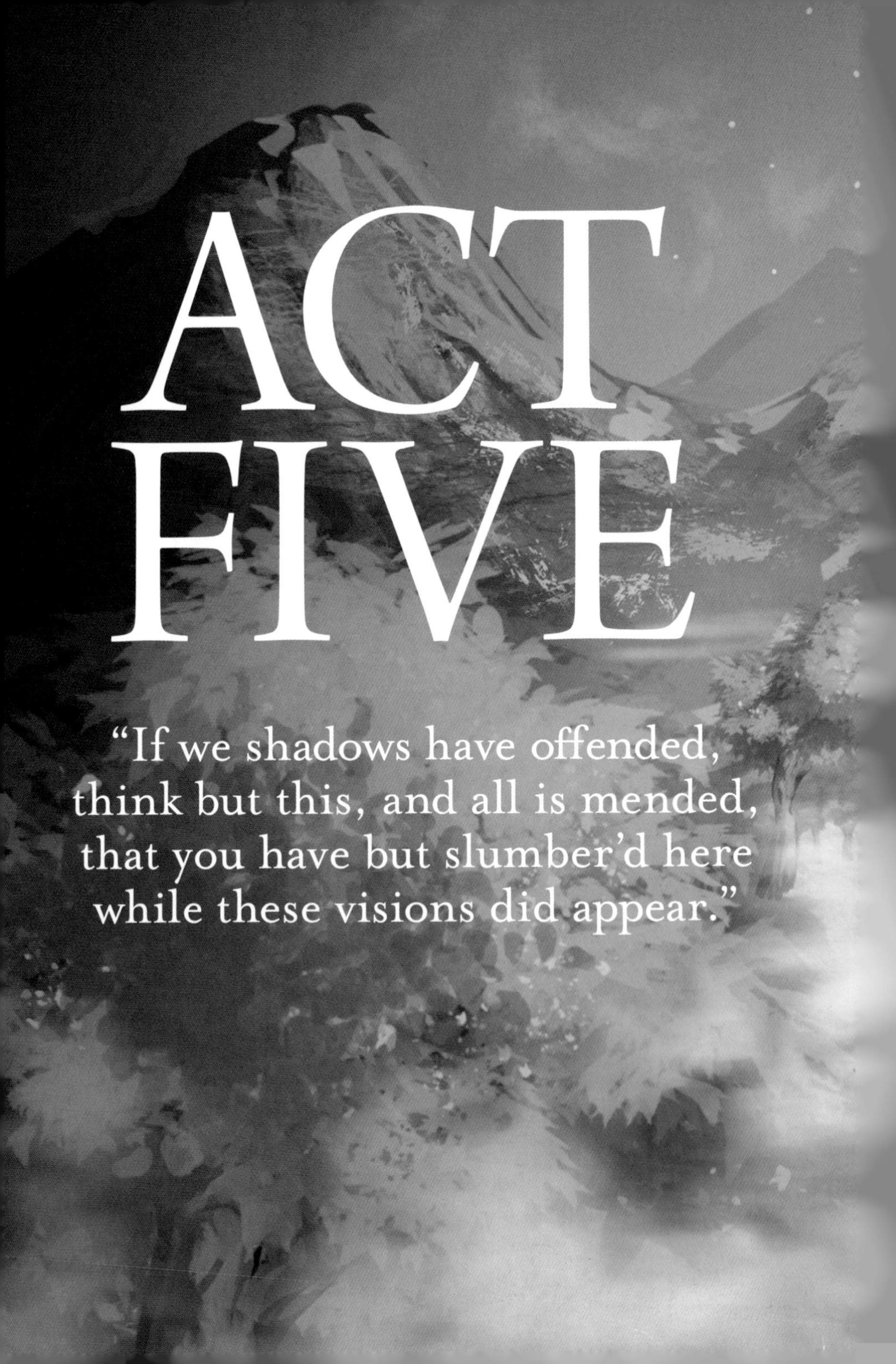

ACT FIVE

"If we shadows have offended,
think but this, and all is mended,
that you have but slumber'd here
while these visions did appear."

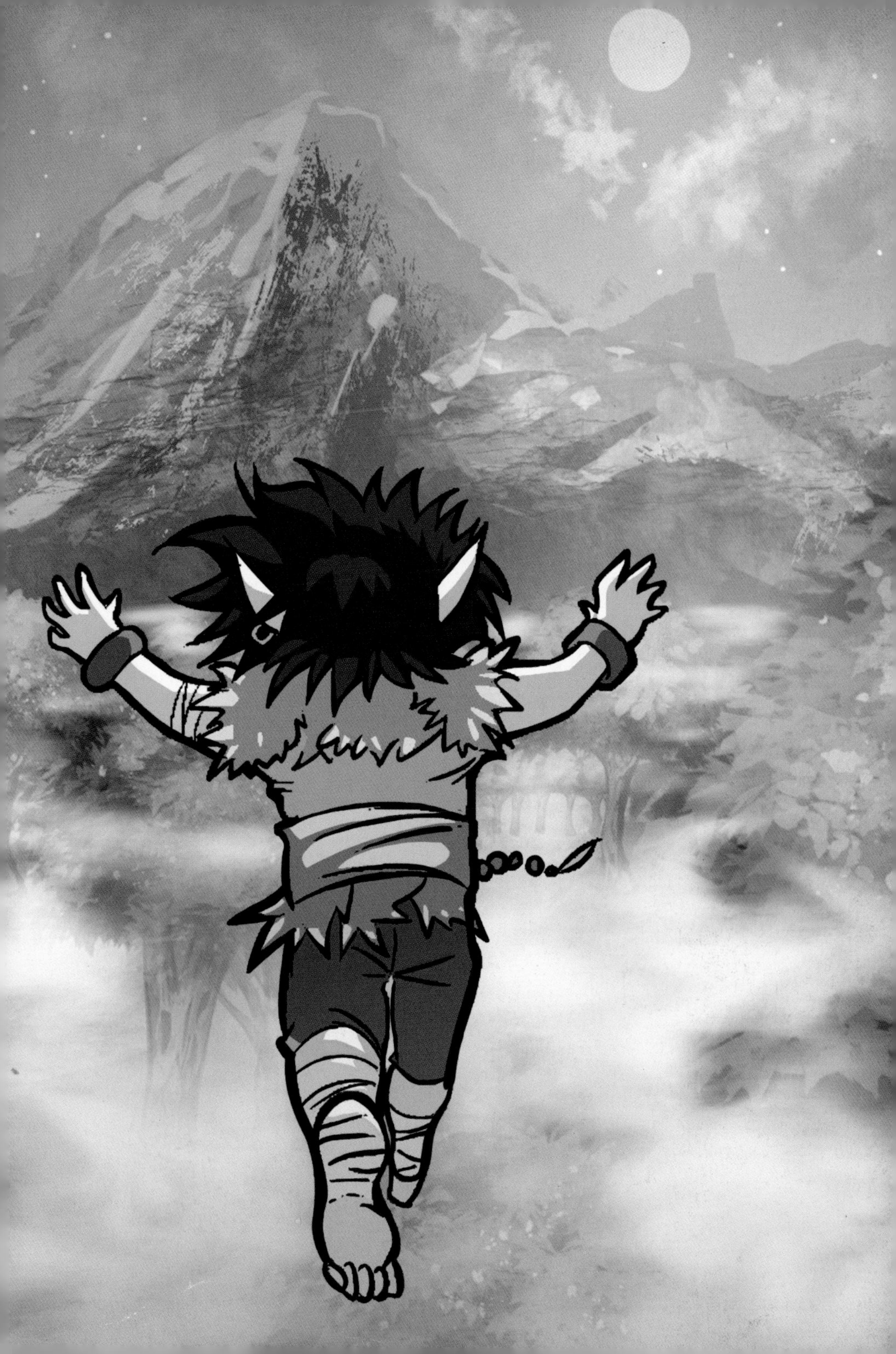

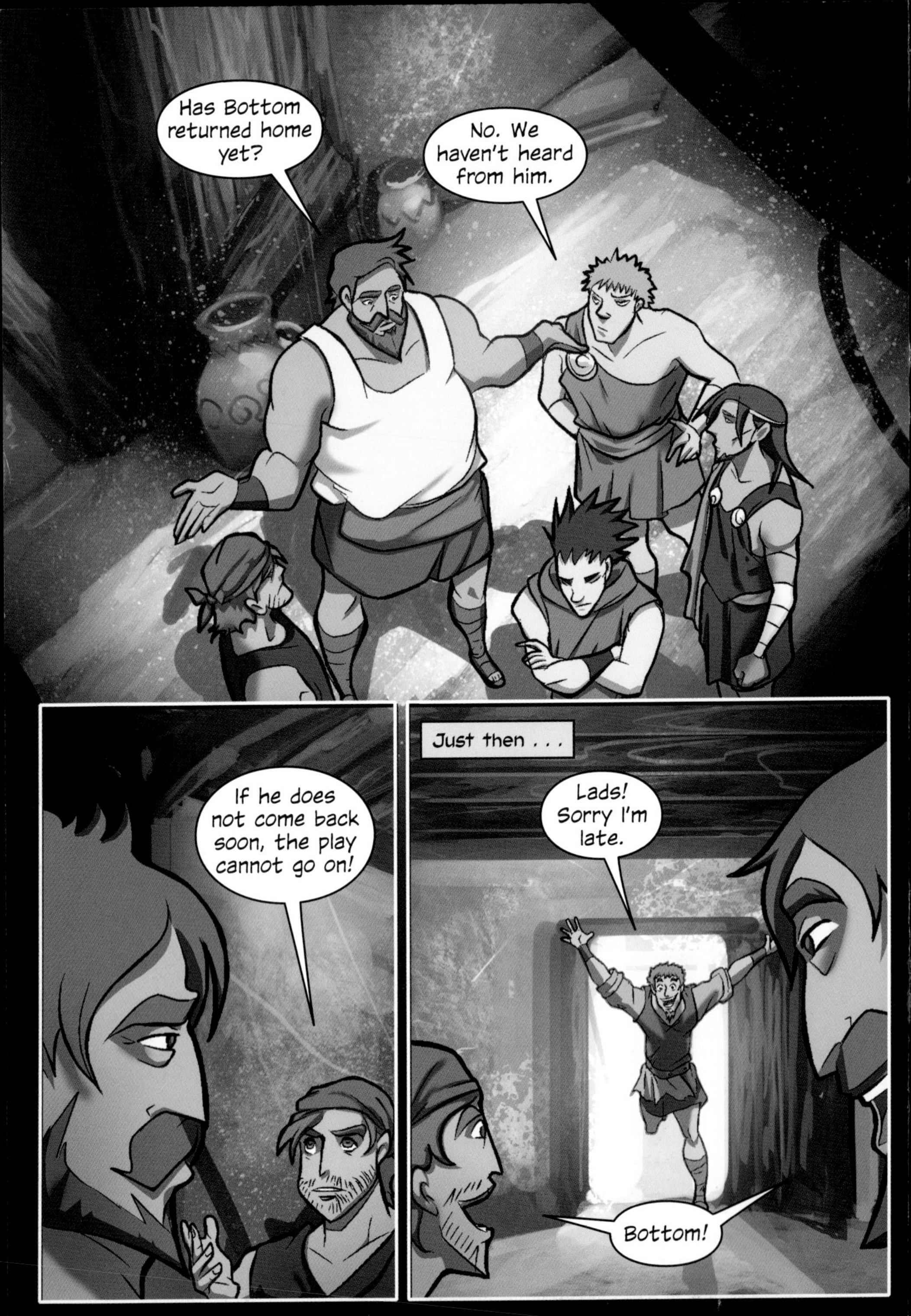
Has Bottom returned home yet?
No. We haven't heard from him.
If he does not come back soon, the play cannot go on!
Just then . . .
Lads! Sorry I'm late.
Bottom!

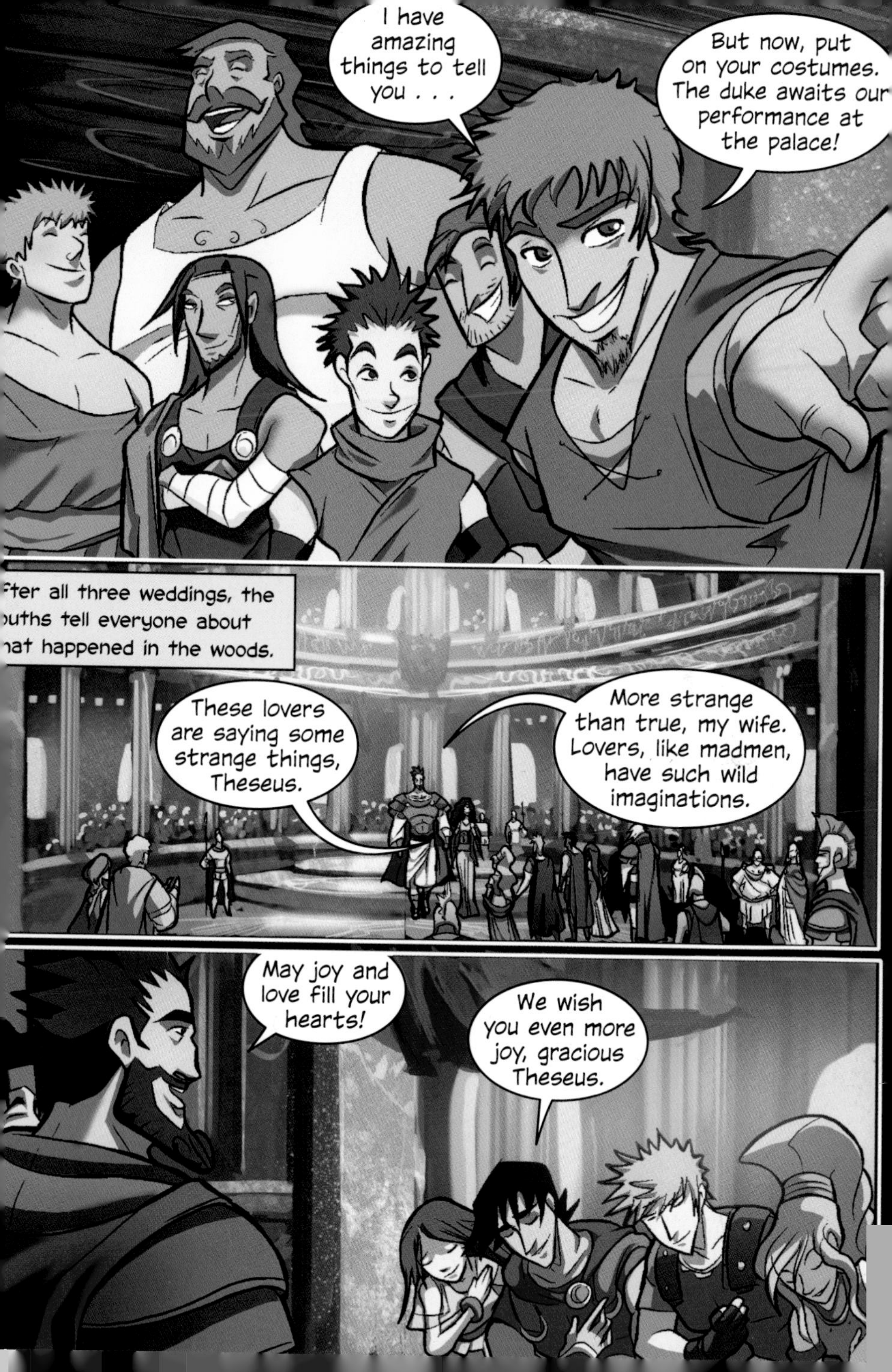
I have amazing things to tell you . . .
But now, put on your costumes. The duke awaits our performance at the palace!
fter all three weddings, the ouths tell everyone about hat happened in the woods.
These lovers are saying some strange things, Theseus.
More strange than true, my wife. Lovers, like madmen, have such wild imaginations.
May joy and love fill your hearts!
We wish you even more joy, gracious Theseus.

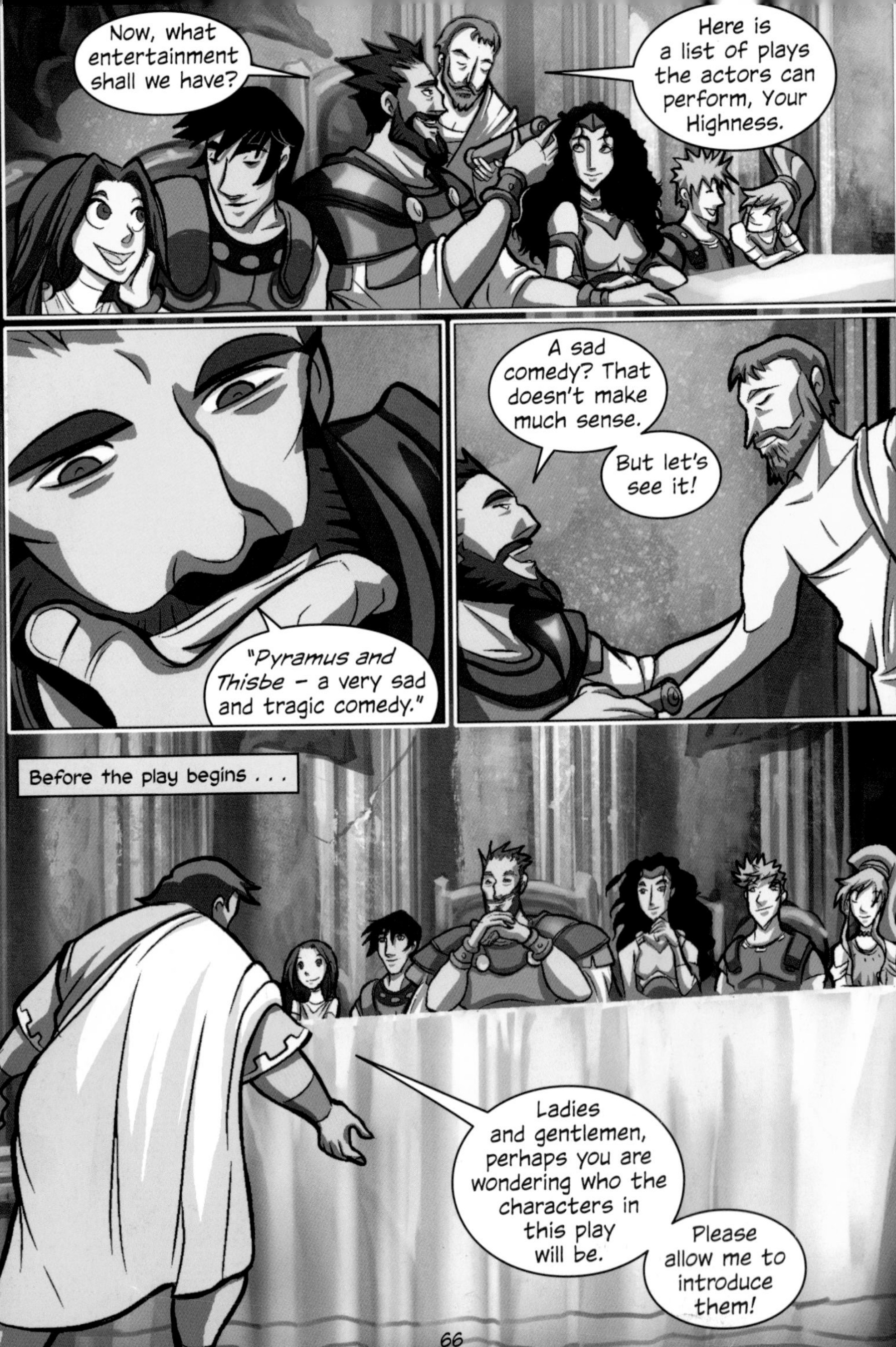

Now, what entertainment shall we have?
Here is a list of plays the actors can perform, Your Highness.
"*Pyramus and Thisbe* – a very sad and tragic comedy."
A sad comedy? That doesn't make much sense.
But let's see it!
Before the play begins . . .
Ladies and gentlemen, perhaps you are wondering who the characters in this play will be.
Please allow me to introduce them!

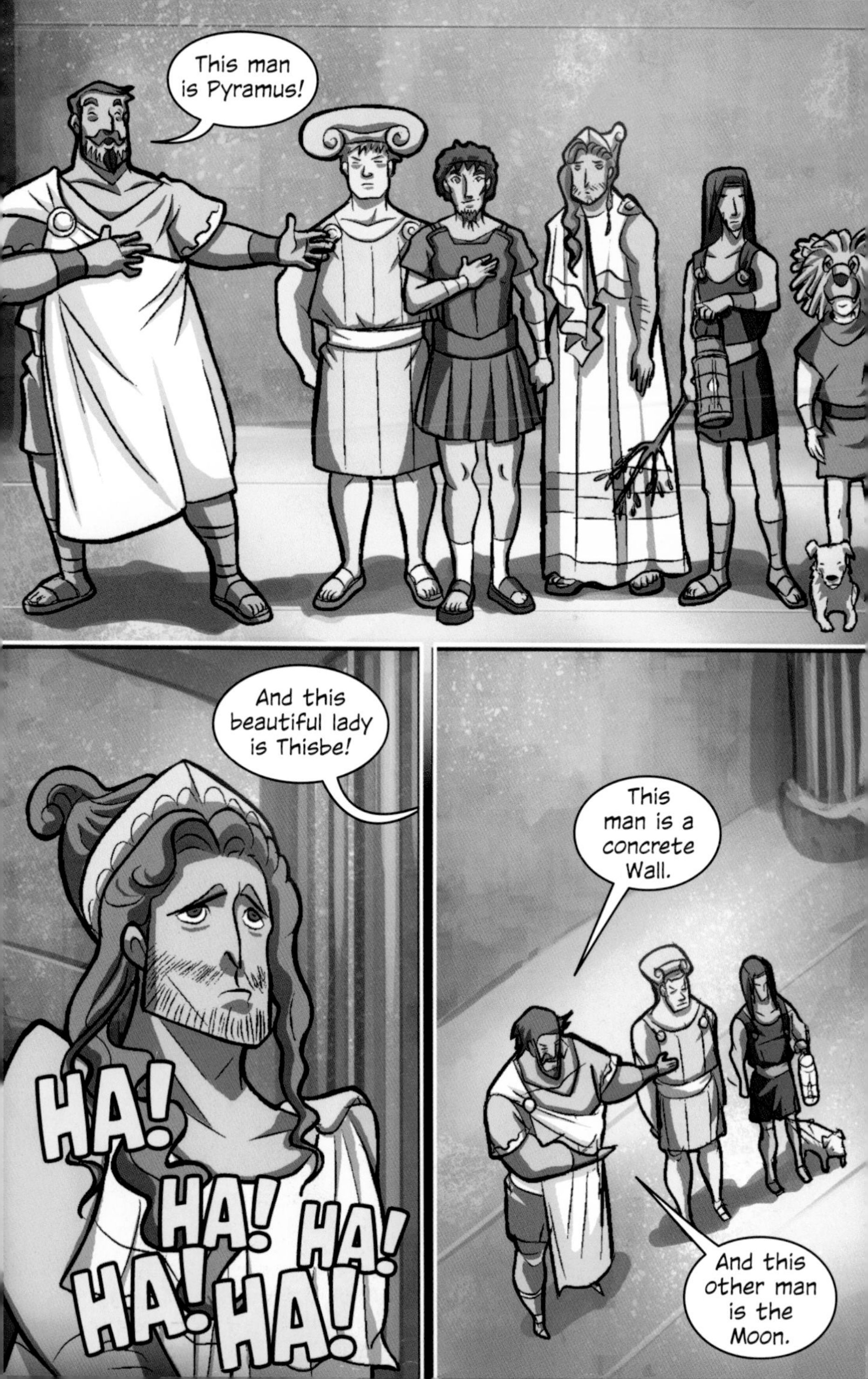
This man is Pyramus!
And this beautiful lady is Thisbe!
HA! HA! HA! HA! HA!
This man is a concrete Wall.
And this other man is the Moon.

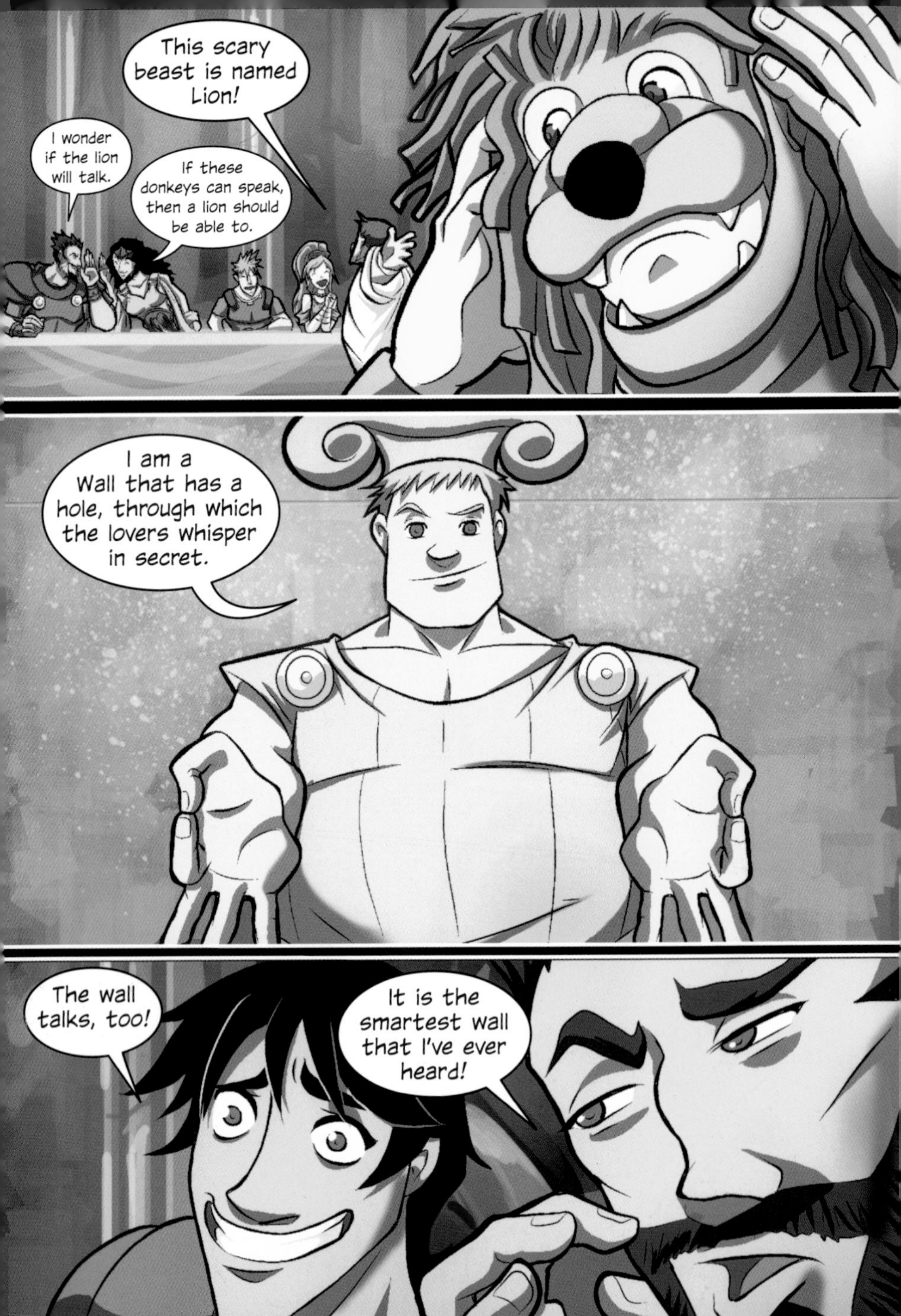

This scary beast is named Lion!
I wonder if the lion will talk.
If these donkeys can speak, then a lion should be able to.
I am a Wall that has a hole, through which the lovers whisper in secret.
The wall talks, too!
It is the smartest wall that I've ever heard!

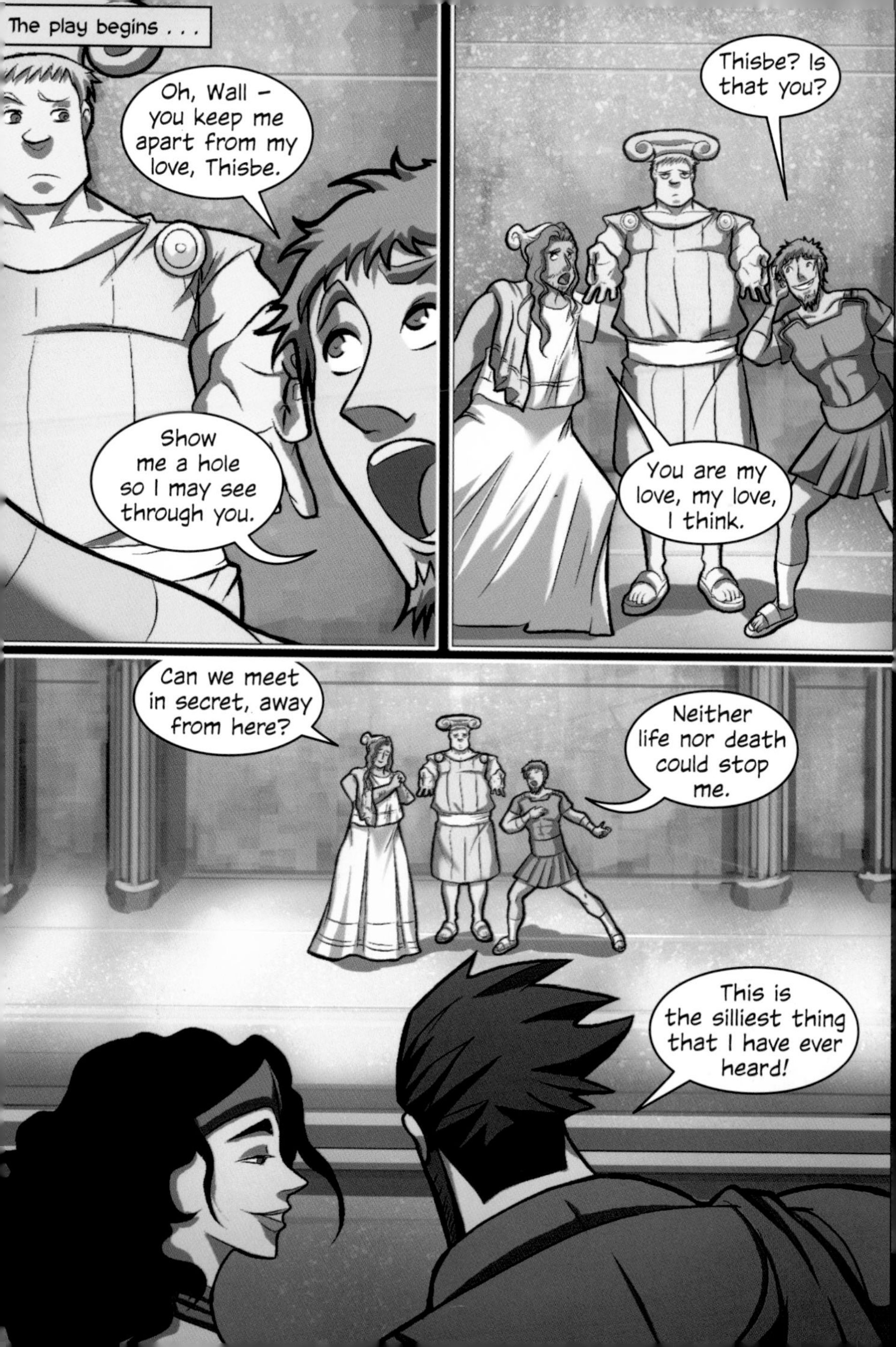
The play begins . . .
Oh, Wall – you keep me apart from my love, Thisbe.
Show me a hole so I may see through you.
Thisbe? Is that you?
You are my love, my love, I think.
Can we meet in secret, away from here?
Neither life nor death could stop me.
This is the silliest thing that I have ever heard!

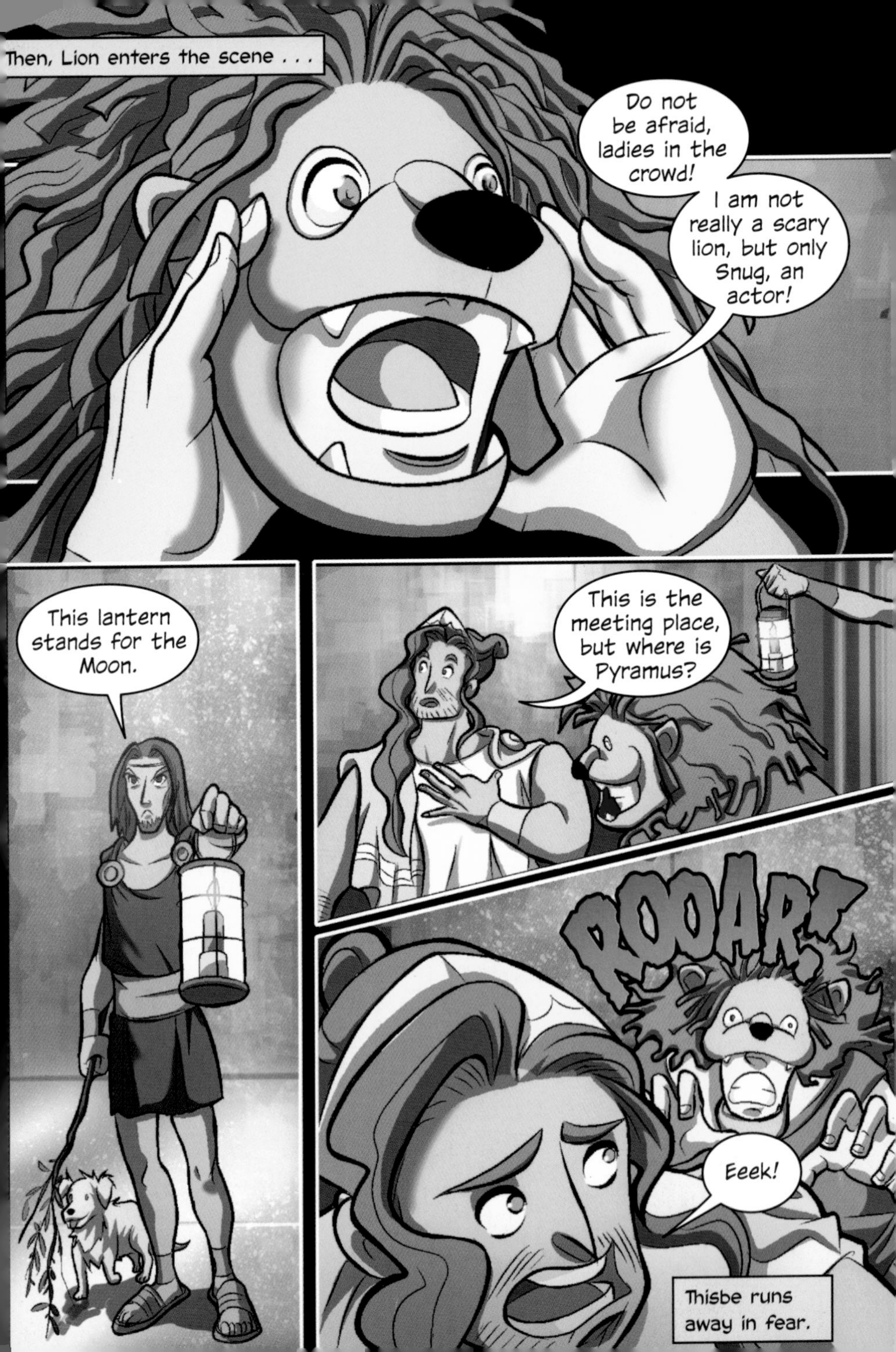
Then, Lion enters the scene . . .
Do not be afraid, ladies in the crowd!
I am not really a scary lion, but only Snug, an actor!
This lantern stands for the Moon.
This is the meeting place, but where is Pyramus?
ROOAR!
Eeek!
Thisbe runs away in fear.

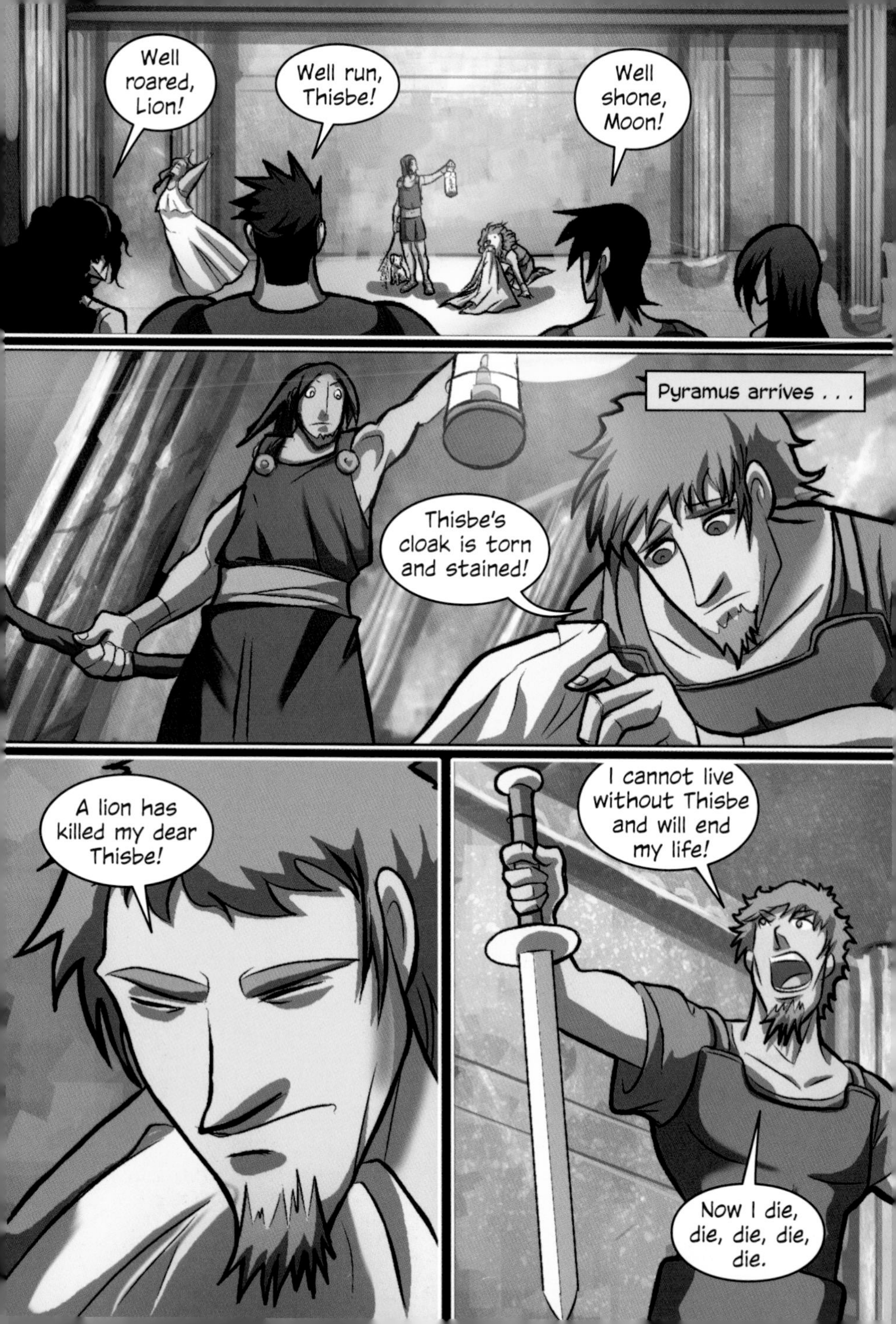
Well roared, Lion!
Well run, Thisbe!
Well shone, Moon!
Pyramus arrives . . .
Thisbe's cloak is torn and stained!
A lion has killed my dear Thisbe!
I cannot live without Thisbe and will end my life!
Now I die, die, die, die, die.

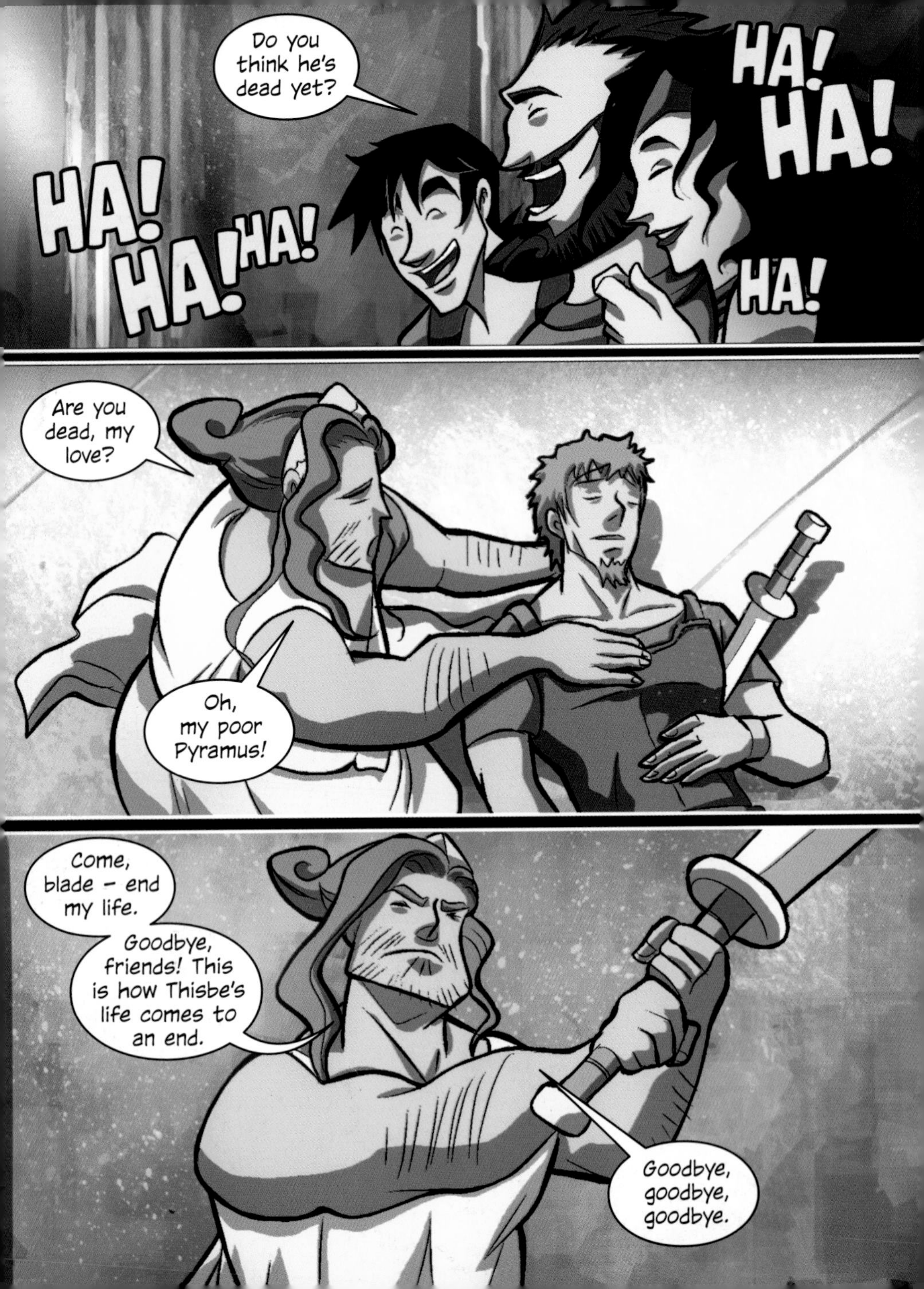
Do you think he's dead yet?
HA! HA!
HA! HA! HA!
HA!
Are you dead, my love?
Oh, my poor Pyramus!
Come, blade – end my life.
Goodbye, friends! This is how Thisbe's life comes to an end.
Goodbye, goodbye, goodbye.

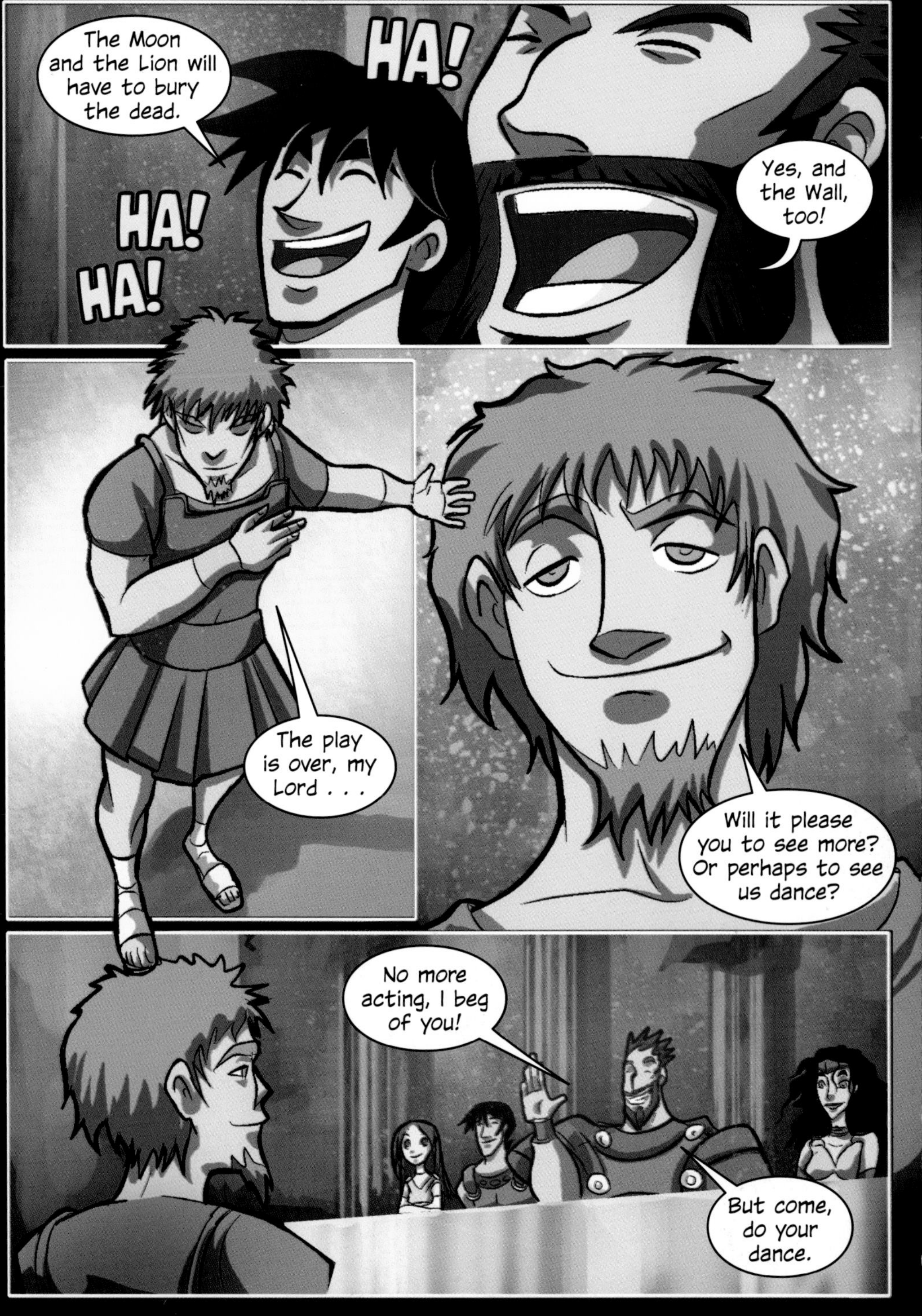
The Moon and the Lion will have to bury the dead.
HA!
HA!
HA!
Yes, and the Wall, too!
The play is over, my Lord . . .
Will it please you to see more? Or perhaps to see us dance?
No more acting, I beg of you!
But come, do your dance.

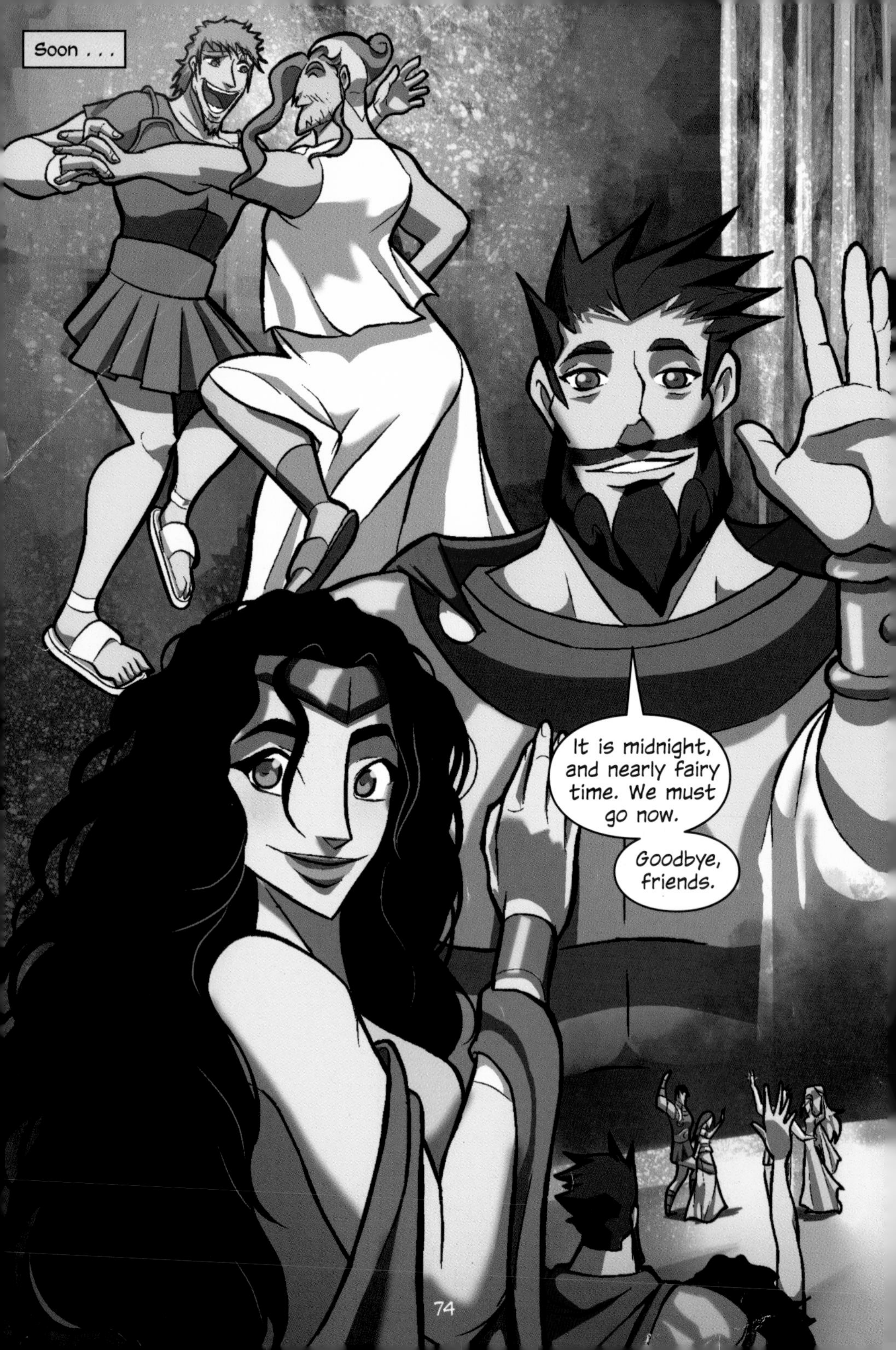
Soon . . .
It is midnight, and nearly fairy time. We must go now.
Goodbye, friends.

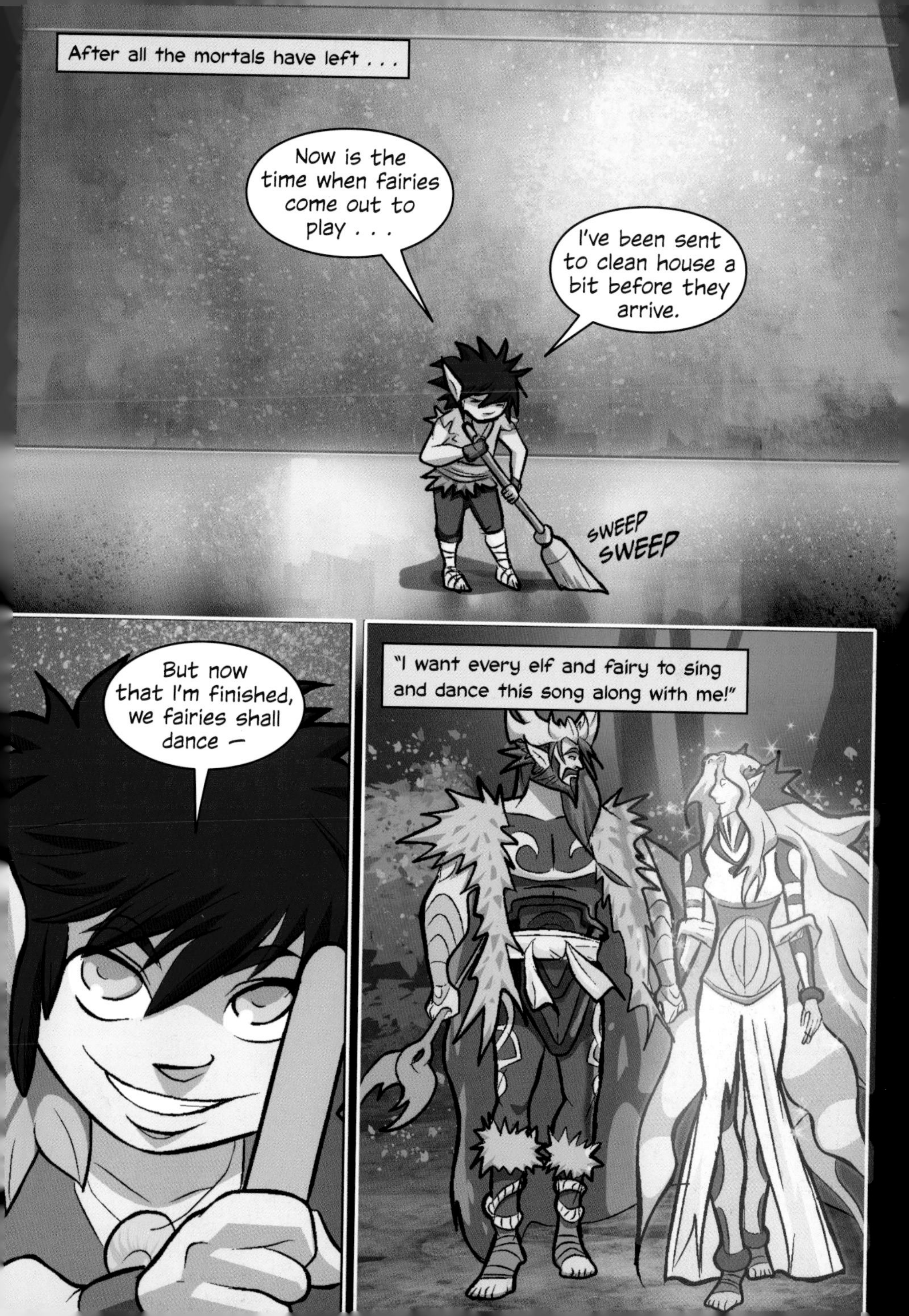
After all the mortals have left . . .
Now is the time when fairies come out to play . . .
I've been sent to clean house a bit before they arrive.
SWEEP SWEEP
But now that I'm finished, we fairies shall dance –
"I want every elf and fairy to sing and dance this song along with me!"

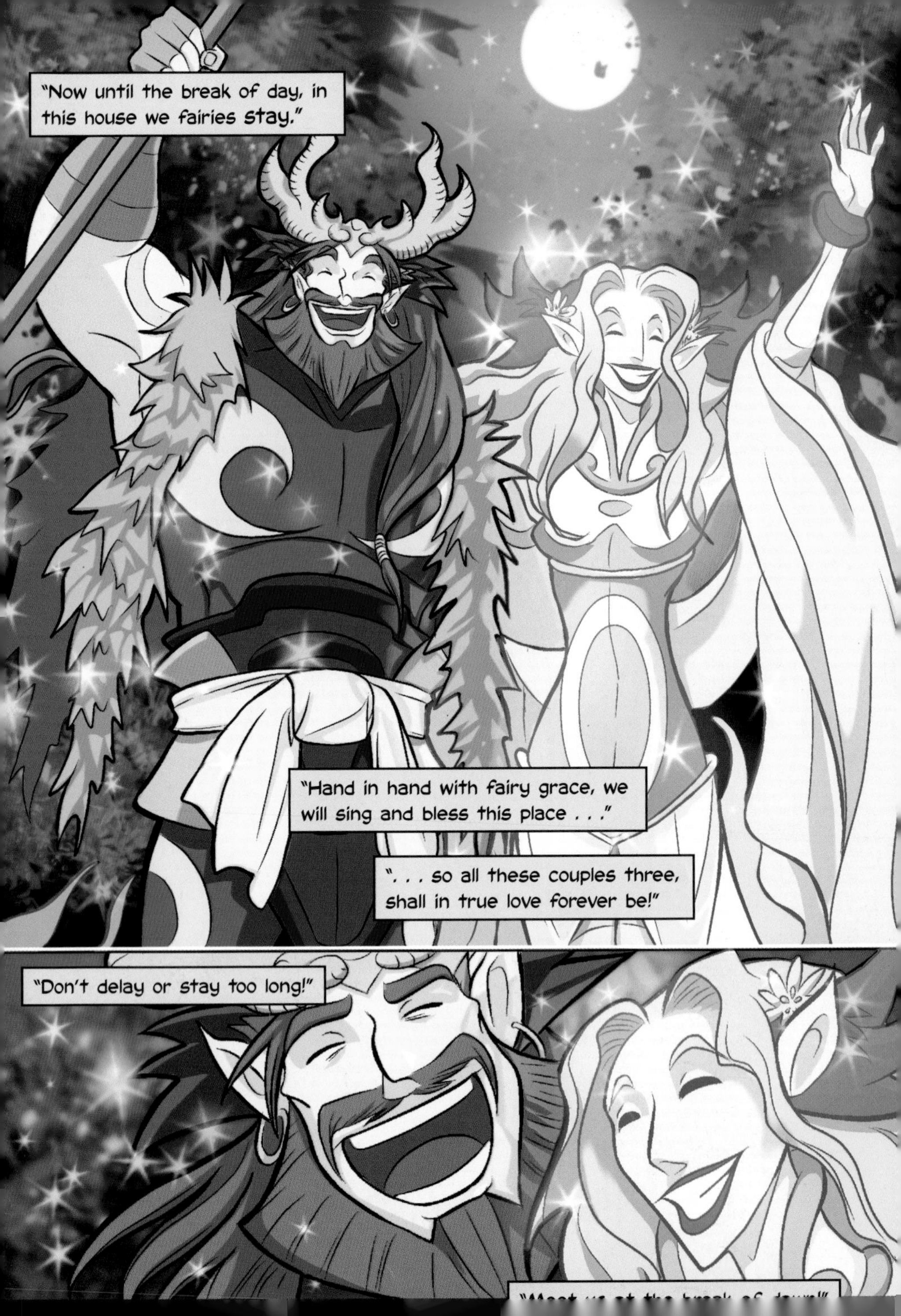
"Now until the break of day, in this house we fairies stay."
"Hand in hand with fairy grace, we will sing and bless this place . . ."
". . . so all these couples three, shall in true love forever be!"
"Don't delay or stay too long!"

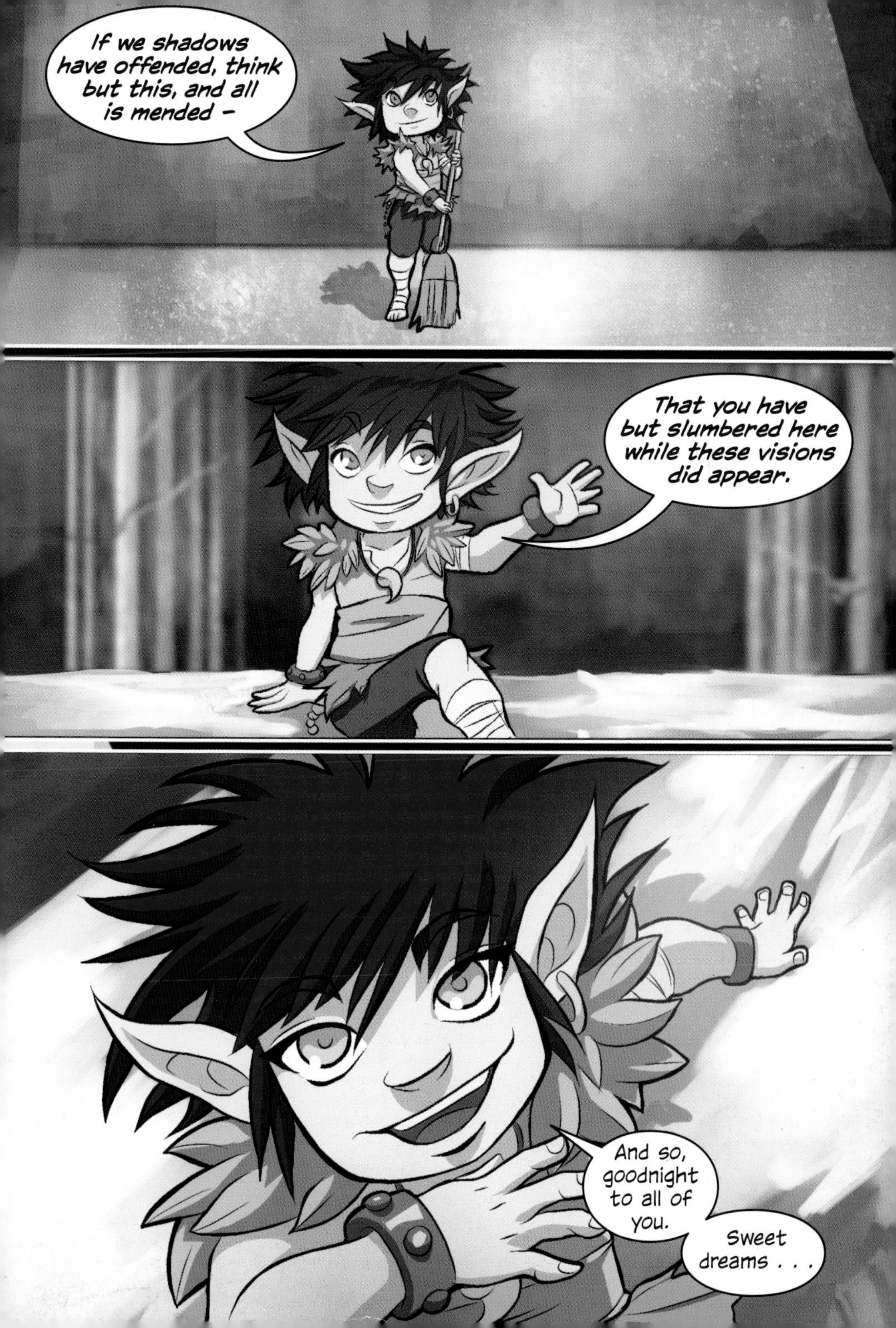
If we shadows have offended, think but this, and all is mended -
That you have but slumbered here while these visions did appear.
And so, goodnight to all of you.
Sweet dreams . . .

ABOUT THE RETELLING AUTHOR

The career path of **Nel Yomtov** has taken him from the halls of Marvel Comics, as an editor, writer, and colorist, to the world of toy development. He then became editorial and art director at a children's nonfiction book publisher, and now Nel is a writer and editor of books, websites, and comics for children. A harmonica-honking blues enthusiast, Nel lives in New York with his wife, Nancy. They have a son, Jess.

ABOUT THE ILLUSTRATORS

Berenice Muniz is a graphic designer and illustrator from Monterrey, Mexico. In the past, she has done work for publicity agencies, art exhibitions, and she's even created her own webcomic. These days, Berenice is devoted to illustrating comics as part of the Graphikslava crew. In her spare time, "Bere" loves to draw, read manga, watch animated movies, play videogames, and kill zombies.

Fares Maese is a graphic designer and illustrator. He has worked as a colorist for Marvel Comics and as a concept artist for the card and role-playing games Pathfinder and Warhammer. Fares loves spending time playing video games with his Graphikslava comrades, and he's an awesome drum player.

ABOUT WILLIAM SHAKESPEARE

William Shakespeare's true date of birth is unknown, but it is celebrated on April 23rd, 1564. He was born in Stratford-upon-Avon, England. He was the third of eight children to his parents, John and Mary.

At age 18, William married a woman named Anne Hathaway on November 27th, 1582. He and Anne had three children together, including twins. After that point, Shakespeare's history is somewhat of a mystery. Not much is known about that period of his life, until 1592 when his plays first graced theater stages in London, England.

From 1594 onward, Shakespeare performed his plays with a stage company called the Lord Chamberlain's Men (later known as the King's Men). They soon became the top playing company in all of London, earning the favor of Queen Elizabeth and King James I along the way.

He retired in 1613, and died at age 52 on April 23rd, 1616. He was buried at Holy Trinity Church in Stratford. The epitaph on his grave curses any person who disturbs it. Translated to modern English, part of it reads:

> *Blessed be the man that spares these stones,*
> *And cursed be he who moves my bones.*

Over a period of 25 years, Shakespeare wrote more than 40 works, including poems, plays, and prose. His plays have been performed all over the world and translated to every major language.

THE HISTORY BEHIND THE PLAY

Shakespeare was inspired by many other works when he wrote *A Midsummer Night's Dream*. For example, the story of *Pyramus and Thisbe*, from Ovid's *Metamorphoses*, played an important role in the creation of Shakespeare's play. It served as a basis for several parts of the play's plot, and is even included in *A Midsummer Night's Dream* as a play-within-a-play! *Pyramus and Thisbe* was also an inspiration for *Romeo and Juliet*, another of Shakespeare's most popular play.

Greek mythology served as a basis for several of the character's names in *A Midsummer Night's Dream*. In Ancient Greek myths, Lysander was a mythological Greek warlord, Theseus was the King of Athens, and Hippolyta was the Queen of the Amazons — a race of fierce, female warriors.

While *A Midsummer Night's Dream* had many inspirations, it has also influenced modern culture. For example, when William Herschel, a British astronomer, discovered the two moons circling the planet Uranus in 1787, he named them Oberon and Titania in honor of the king and queen of the fairies.

No one knows for certain when *A Midsummer Night's Dream* was first written or performed. Nevertheless, the play has been performed across the globe for hundreds of years. It has also been recreated as musicals, operas, ballets, books, movies — and graphic novels like this one.

SHAKESPEAREAN LANGUAGE

Shakespeare's writing is powerful and memorable — and sometimes difficult to understand. Many lines in his plays can be read in different ways or can have multiple meanings. Also, the English language was not standardized in Shakespeare's time, so the way he spelled words was not always the same as we spell them nowadays. However, Shakespeare still influences the way we write and speak today. Below are some of his more famous phrases that have become part of our language.

FAMOUS LINES FROM A MIDSUMMER NIGHT'S DREAM

"The course of true love never did run smooth." (Act I, Scene I)

SPEAKER: Lysander

MODERN INTERPRETATION: **True love always faces obstacles.**

EXPLANATION: Lysander explains to Hermia that being in love is always difficult because so many things have to be considered when two lovers want to be married.

"I am that merry wanderer of the night." (Act II, Scene I)

SPEAKER: Puck (Robin Goodfellow)

MODERN INTERPRETATION: **That's me, I am the playful Robin Goodfellow, also known as Puck.**

EXPLANATION: Puck, a playful fairie-sprite, plays tricks on others on Oberon's behalf. Puck identifies himself formally as Robin Goodfellow, but most fairies know him simply as Puck.

"And yet, to say the truth, reason and love keep little company together nowadays." (Act III, Scene I)

SPEAKER: Bottom

MODERN INTERPRETATION: **To tell you the truth, logic and love rarely go hand in hand these days.**

EXPLANATION: Titania, under a spell of love, falls in love with Bottom at first sight. Bottom, not knowing he has the head of a donkey, remarks that she has no reason to love him. He then adds that, lately, love hasn't been making much sense at all.

"I have had a dream, past the wit of man to say what dream it was." (Act IV, Scene I)

SPEAKER: Bottom

MODERN INTERPRETATION: **I was dreaming! My dream was so strange that I couldn't even explain it if I tried.**

EXPLANATION: Bottom wakes up without his donkey head, and thinks that the entire experience of falling in love with Titania was only a dream.

"If we shadows have offended, think but this, and all is mended, that you have but slumber'd here while these visions did appear." (Act V, Scene I)

SPEAKER: Puck

MODERN INTERPRETATION: **If you, the viewer, did not like anything that happened in this play, then relax — it was all just your dream.**

EXPLANATION: Puck breaks the "fourth wall" and speaks directly to the audience of the play. He tells them that they should not worry if they were offended, or they did not like what they saw during the play, because they only dreamt the whole thing.

DISCUSSION QUESTIONS

1. Of all the characters in *A Midsummer Night's Dream*, which one was your favorite? Why?

2. This play is considered to be a comedy. Did you think it was funny? Why or why not?

3. Do think Theseus was a fair ruler in this book? What about King Oberon? What makes for a good ruler?

1. Magic and spells are used to distract, confuse, and control characters in this book. Think up a magic spell of your own. What does it do? How do you cast it? Write about your spell. Then draw a picture of your spell in action.

2. In the play, Oberon and Titania fight over an Indian boy. In Shakepseare's time, fairies were said to steal children and keep them as servants. Imagine that you are kidnapped by fairies for a day. Write about your experiences as the son or daughter of a fairy king and queen.

3. The performance of *Pyramus and Thisbe* in *A Midsummer Night's Dream* is called a play-within-a-play. Write your own one-page play, including several characters, a story, and dialogue.

NTRODUCING ANOTHER SHAKESPEARE GRAPHIC NOVE

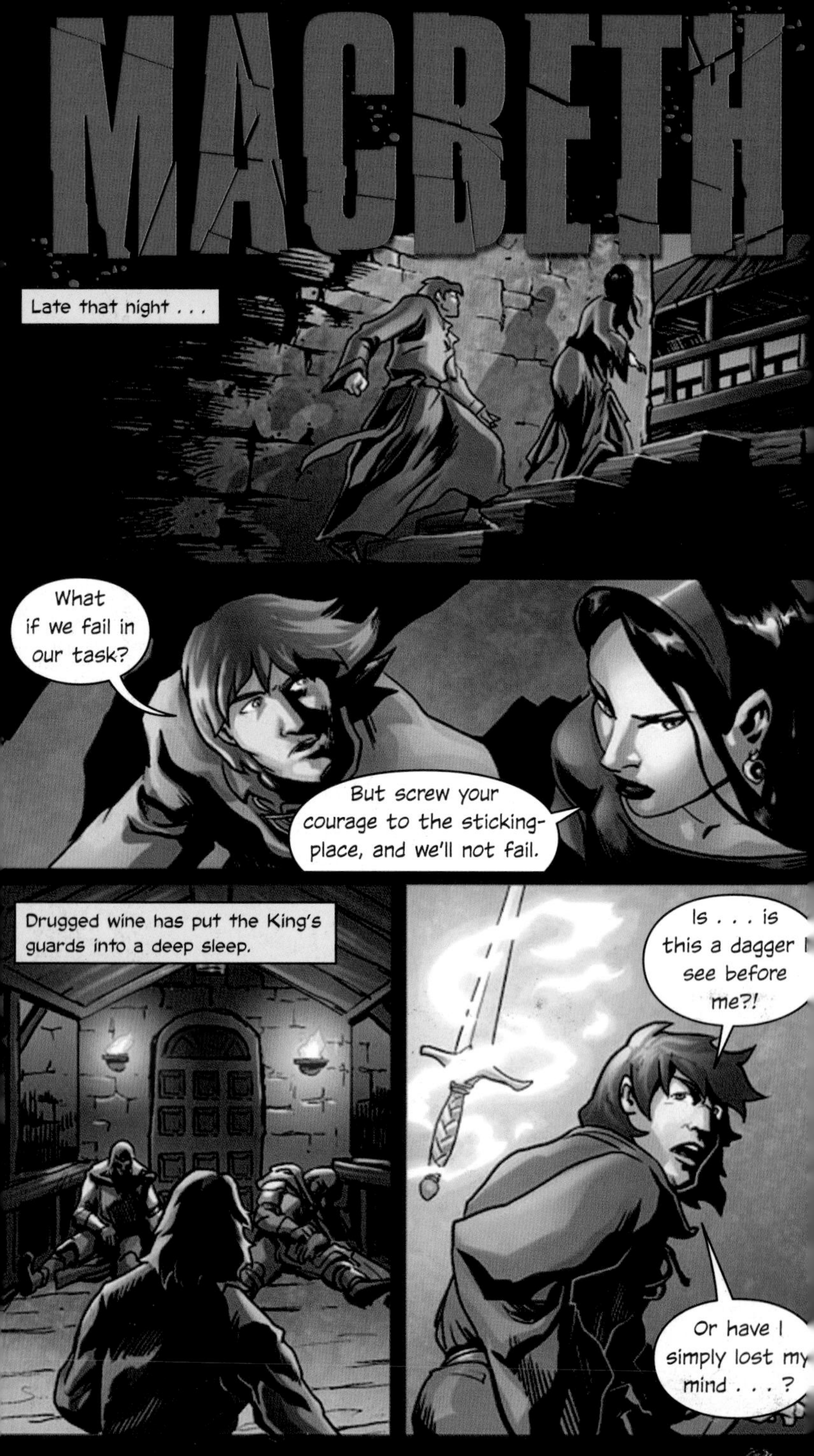
MACBETH
Late that night . . .
What if we fail in our task?
But screw your courage to the sticking-place, and we'll not fail.
Drugged wine has put the King's guards into a deep sleep.
Is . . . is this a dagger I see before me?!
Or have I simply lost my mind . . . ?

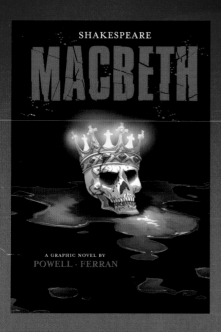
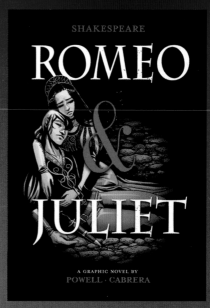
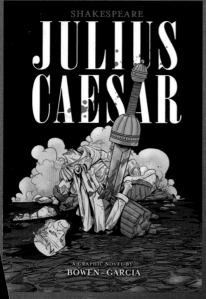
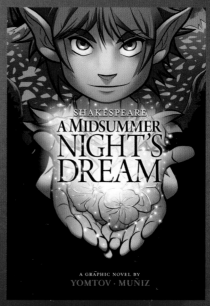

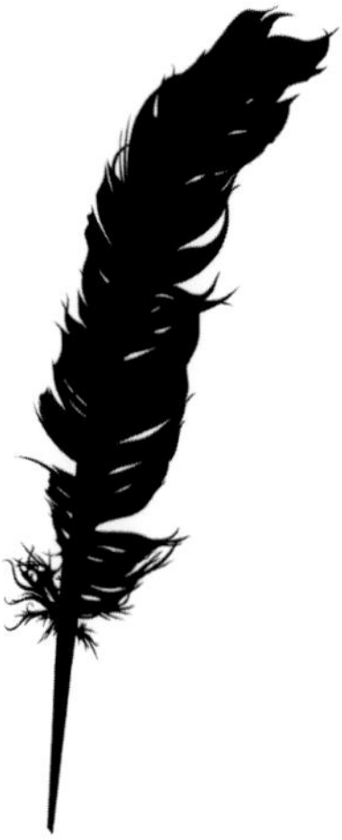

"ALL THE WORLD'S A STAGE."

— WILLIAM SHAKESPEARE

WWW.CAPSTONEPUB.COM